Orb of Wonders

Orb of Wonders

By Mill Woods

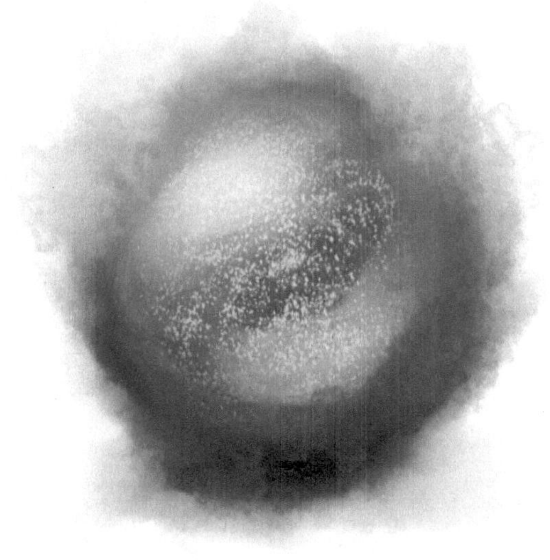

ISBN: 978-87-971819-4-2
Printed version 3 (2024)

Prologue

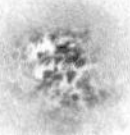

A little society full of dreaming children; Some of their dreams revealed the future. Others processed the past. A sleeping grandfather thought his dreams to be biological simulations, training and preparing the mind for dangerous situations. The neighbor thought them to be random imagination. A teenage daughter urged for them to be exposures of other levels, dimensions or realities. Could she control her dreams? Or even let them become her reality?

The little society still needed time before evidence would be discovered. Until then, dreams could be anything they wished for.

Chapter 1

Another drop of boiling blood ran down the cracks in my glasses. What happened? The flashlight on the ground illuminated only the area in front of me, revealing the small pool of wine-colored substance dripping from my head. Everything else was dark and quiet.

I removed the broken glasses and found that my eyes were seeing clear as never before. Still, my vision was filled with glare from the light source, like switching on a light in a dark bedroom; Blinding. I had no clue how long I had been lying unconscious in the cold, humid space, and I was shivering heavily, frozen to the bones. All I knew was that my daughter needed me.

I managed to drag myself up from the rocky ground and picked up the flashlight. *What the hell?* The bodies of three young people were spread out around me. None of them alive, all surrounded by black marks of blood. In an attempt to find any clues, I conquered my dismay and searched each of the corpses, but found nothing. Nothing but that god damned wondrous orb rolling out the hand of the dead female. I didn't reflect much upon it when picking it up and putting it in my pocket.

With the flashlight in my hand, I illuminated parts of the black space; Large marble monuments of terrifying cat- and ape-like creatures, with tiny pupils of black rock, were placed in a circle around me. Their presence penetrated my stomach with freezing anxiety, why my lungs felt as being burned with every inhale.

Some of the creatures held golden pieces of jewelry decorated with gems of various colors. Others held objects like books or fabrics. One particular monument sat with an enormous clock made from glossy ebony, with shiny golden hands and ornaments, yet the mechanism was stuck. Besides all of these monuments, only walls of spiky rock were present. Above, I saw from where we had fallen. Only wings could get me back up there, but I knew that I had to get out, somehow. She needed me. I should be with her. That I remembered.

A noise sounded from one end of the cavernous space. My flashlight revealed a passage, and my ears prepared me for an unknown visitor, which didn't seem human. The noise reminded me of two sprinting hooves echoing rapidly through the passage, along with deep inhales and hollow exhales. I panicked. Instantly, I hid behind one of the monuments and killed the flashlight. The creature was in the room already, and the heavy breathing was nearing. I glanced over the monument. Even in the lack of light, I saw the tiny, white pupils, hovering in the black space, flickering in the search for something. It inspected the dead bodies, but they weren't the targets. I heard its massive claws move fast, as it started crawling around, examining the ground while letting out horrifying cries; It lost something; I recognized that feeling. Before I knew it, the creature was right beside me. I could smell its decaying breath, like acid to my nostrils. I put a hand to my mouth and held my breath to avoid making any sounds - and avoid puking from the rotten stink. Drops of warm liquid found its way into my eyes, painfully blinding me from the dark, yet I wasn't sure if it was sweat, blood or saliva from the creature. Nevertheless, I prepared to experience my death.

"Sit still," an echoing whisper commanded.

Without questioning the whisperer, I did as told. I sat there for twenty minutes before the creature returned out through the passage. I sat there even ten minutes more, just to be sure. The darkness and silence was overwhelming.

"It is gone," the whisper informed.

This time the whispering was right behind my ear, and goosebumps appeared. With shaking hands and trembling breaths, I dared to turn on the flashlight. It took a few inhales to find strength before I slowly moved my head around to face the whisperer, but no one was there.

"We are alone now," the whispering continued.

"Who..." I mumbled. "Who are *we*?"

This time the reply came from my pocket; A silent laughter. I moved my shaking hand down and picked up the orb. That god damned extraordinary orb. A purple glow ignited within. It was alluring like nothing I'd never seen before. Out of words, I stared at the thing for hours, just waiting for it to whisper to me again.

"It's time," it finally whispered. "Find peace."

dream

The alarm clock managed to play its shrill tones nine times before I punched it mute with my half-dead arm. As usual, I sneaked out the bed and slid my way to the door, careful not to wake Mona. In the kitchen, I swallowed my vitamins, added the usual two teaspoons of instant coffee to my usual, brown mug, and as usual, I filled the mug only halfway with boiled water.

Standing in the living room by the morning-sunny window, enjoying my black brew, I checked the ticking clock on the wall: 07.25. That meant that there was less than one minute until... Yes, there he was... That stupid neighbor in his god damned red training suit, jogging with a smoking cigarette in his mouth. How I hated that guy. I hated everything about him. I hated his annoying, bald face, with that smart-ass smirk he always wore when repeatedly telling about his one-time trip to Dubai. I hated his rusty front yard sprinklers, sounding like gunshots every time they turned on. I hated his braindead wife with all of her constant nonsense babbling when meeting her on the street. I just hated everything about that guy.

The wall clock played its "half-past" tone. That meant... Ah, yes, there she was! My little princess.

"Good morning, dad!" Violet shouted with that beautiful smile she always wore.

"Good morning, little shark," I replied, as I knew how much she loved me calling her sea animal names.

She hugged me tight, just like she did every morning. My smile was forced wide and genuine - I just couldn't help it. I always feared the day she would grow old enough to stop completing my day, in advance, with morning hugs like those.

Moments later, Mona came down the stairs, like always, yawning with her dark hair floating in all directions.

"Morning, love," she always said with her English accent before heading off to the kitchen.

"Morning, honey." I always managed to reply.

I took a look at my little Violet.

"I like what you did to your hair," I said and stroke the blue lines she dyed in cooperation with her mother last night.

It suited her long, blond fairy-hair flawlessly.

"Thanks, Dad!" she replied with a grin. "Mom dyed her hair too! Did you see?"

I'd always found Violet's energy-level inspiring. Her big, blue eyes sparkled with joy all day long. How she got those cheerful blue eyes is still a mystery, as both Mona and I had coffee brown eyes, and always had. My mother had blue eyes, so I assumed the eye-color simply skipped a generation.

"Yes, I noticed, little dolphin," I replied. "It suits your mother too, but not as much as you."

She giggled.

"You're silly, Dad."

As usual, while Mona had her coffee in the kitchen, I helped Violet get ready for school. I helped her pack her books. I helped her remember her lunch box. I made sure she brushed her teeth - because, you know, a princess needs her teeth shining. Today I was allowed to help her decide whether she should wear the green socks with strawberries or the blue ones with watermelons. I chose the blue ones, of course. Some people found these things to be hard duties, but I enjoyed every minute; Until the wall clock played its tone. It was time. I had to leave for work. I hated that "eight o'clock" tone. I hated leaving Violet. And I hated placing myself in that rubber-wheeled metal box and drive off to work. But I had to; Money never came flying with the wind.

"See you tonight, Dad!" Violet shouted from the window as I closed the front door behind me.

It was Tuesday, so I knew exactly what she meant.

"See you tonight, little seahorse."

Chapter 2

I roamed for some time, examining the strange monuments with all of their golden treasures. No matter how hard I tried remembering, nothing in here brought my memory back. The orb didn't say anything, letting me wonder on my own. I inspected every little thing in the area. I ran a finger over the rough fabric of a folded blanket, lying at the feet of what looked like a petrified hyena. As my finger reached the end, a thumb-sized grey spider, with long, thin legs, crawled up my hand. In a panic, I shook it off and jumped back. I hated insects! I *hated* spiders! For the next ten minutes, I searched the ground for the spider, but it was nowhere to be seen. I feared that it had landed on me somewhere, but I didn't find it on my body either. Maybe I was just hallucinating and claustrophobic. I had to get out of there - now.

Apparently, there was only one way out: through the passage in which the creature left. I felt trapped and alone in the dark, mysterious cave - especially with dead bodies lying on the ground, watching me in their silence. Staring back didn't quite help.

"You wonder about the past," the whispering suggested.

I picked up the orb from my pocket and watched its glow.

"Why don't I remember anything?" I asked. "Who are those people?"

The orb returned low laughter before replying.

"Time will tell, friend. Don't worry."

"What do you mean?" I asked.

The orb didn't reply.

"Can you tell me where I am?" I tried asking.

"Time will tell, friend. Time will tell."

In confusion, I stared at the mesmerizing thing, trying to figure out what the hell it meant. *Time will tell?* Was I just supposed to wait here for answers? I couldn't do that! I had to get out to my daughter. She needed me. There was nothing I could do but go through that passage. I picked up a relic from one of the monuments, ready to use it as a weapon, in case I should reencounter the creature. The relic was heavy, and though I couldn't recognize the object, I was certain that this was a gold plated coconut from ancient times. How I knew was a mystery in itself.

"Wait," the orb whispered as I was about to enter the passage. "Didn't you want to know what happened here?"

I sighted.

"Let me guess. Will time tell?" I suggested.

"True. But first, consider how you spend that time."

I stayed mute.

"Think about the past," it continued. "You can't change the past."

"And what is that supposed to mean?"

"You can't change your past, but you can control what you add to it."

"How so?"

"With the moment you're experiencing now, you're adding to your past."

I clenched my fist, feeling the frustration come.

"And why are you telling me this?" I asked.

"I am simply reminding you, that your current choices are more important than the past, friend."

"I don't get it."

"Does it change what you're about to do if you know what happened in this place?"

"Well, it might."

"Does it change your emotions if you remember who you were before this place?"

"It might."

"Does it change your current longings if you know what happened before you ended up here?"

This time I didn't reply. The orb laughed silently again.

"I'm not trying to confuse you. Just consider what you add to your past. Bad decisions in the moment will transfer to that past."

"Bad decisions? Did I kill these people?"

"Can you change the past?" it asked.

"I guess not," I replied.

"Then, don't worry about it."

Again, I stayed mute, reflecting.

"Listen," it continued. "The past tells you who you were, what you were doing. The moment tells you who you are, what you are doing. The future tells you who you will become, what you will do. You can't change the past, but you can change the moment and your future. Now consider which is least important."

I was baffled. At that moment, I merely understood any of this nonsense - expect the point that the past wasn't changing my longings; All I wanted was getting out to my daughter, no matter how I ended up here. However, somewhere inside me, I knew that all the words were true. What was that orb anyway, trying to fill me with strange knowledge? Something prevented me from asking questions about that. When I tried speaking questions about the origin and meaning of the orb, my words didn't reach. In the end I gave up, for now. Questions could wait.

"I need to get out," I commanded.
"Of course, friend. I am here for you."

dream

The clock in my office sounded its gong. My lunch break, including a chair power nap, was over. I had to get back to that ridiculous guard work now. As usual, I placed my cheap glasses on my nose and glanced at the dusty archaeology books on the shelf in the corner. I never dared to read them. Shouldn't I have accepted by now that it was too late? I would never become an archeologist. My life's dream was never going to be fulfilled. When I applied for this horrible guard job, around the time Violet was born, I thought it would inspire me to start studying. I had this idea that being surrounded by all these ancient objects would do the job. Working in an archaeology museum would be the perfect entry point for my future carrier. Now I was stuck with that low-income job where nothing ever happened, constantly being reminded of what I missed out on, envying the archeologists' research and their work in the facility. Even if anything ever happened on the job, I would have no idea how to react. I didn't know about conflict management. I was just there for the view, being *the presence of a security guard.*

As I stood up from my chair, my security name tag dropped from my vest. I picked it up and took a sad look at it. The image had faded a bit over the six years of working here. I had a bit more hair back then. The skin was not as wrinkled and pale. The smile was genuine and significant, as Violet was just born.

"Christian Hawkin. What happened to you?" I heard myself

mumble.

With the name tag attached, I left my office. The door to the neighbor room was open, and I stopped to overhear the three geeks discuss how to calculate the update rate of the world. As usual, I didn't understand half of what they talked about, with their silly, nerdy words and obscure understanding of the universe. I peeked inside to see the two males sit still, intensely tapping on their calculators, while the female roamed around, babbling, in her strange, thin toe-shoes. Didn't they have real work to do? What were they even doing around here? I never dared to ask - or to speak to most people around here for that matter. People were looking down on me in my role as a security guard. They didn't know about my passion for archaeology, and I was ashamed to tell them. I found my place as a background security guard pretty quickly, just silently roaming the museum, not disturbing the more important people. I never wanted that, but now it was too late.

A group of loudly amused children entered the lobby of the museum. I found my way there to watch them, making sure they saw me as well. The mood instantly lowered as I stepped inside the lobby. I tried smiling at one of the kids who glanced my way, but he turned his head away, ignoring me. The educator of the museum led the kids to the *"newly discovered treasures"* room and started explaining. I had heard the speech before, secretly absorbing all the information I could. The children didn't seem as interested. Two of the boys found their way out of the group and started playing near the glass case with bronze rings. Something inside me hoped for them to push each other, tip over the glass case and create an explosion of a thousand tiny fractions of glass and bronze, even though I knew the rings were irreplaceable. I just wanted *something* to happen. Just for once. However, I ended up clearing my throat and correcting my glasses to indicate that the boys should calm down, and let them know that the grumpy guard was watching. After all, I had a deep respect for these archaelogical findings.

Chapter 3

I ran the fastest I could. The god damned thing was right behind me, chasing me, trying to grab out for my shirt. I smelled its rotten breath. I sensed its needle-teeth preparing to penetrate me. The gasps for air created a hollow noise through its trachea, and the lungs were filled with liquid. I feared the moment I would trip and let the thing devour me, and I was almost out of energy. Still, I managed to speed up, feeling my heart pump like crazy, outrunning the creature a slight bit, with fright and panic.

"Here, turn right," the orb whispered. "Hide behind the monument and turn off your flashlight."

I did as the orb commanded. Again, sitting surrounded by darkness, I could do nothing but wait. The creature ran right past me, sending me a blow of air from its sprinting movement. Its howls echoed into the passage. Screams and cries replied to its howling from the deep. They were hunting for me - all of them. I would never get out of this place alive. I considered ending the upcoming suffering right away - just reveal myself and get it over with. The volume of the howls and cries increased. This was it. I stood up, ready to feed the creatures. I took a step forward, but then the sounds stopped. Everything was silent. *What the...?*

"They are planning," the orb informed.

I brought it to my hand and saw the light glow even brighter than before, shifting between blue and green hues, pulsing, with bright particles floating inside. A bit of time passed before I could remove my eyes. It always did.

"What are they planning?" I managed to ask.

"They don't want us to leave."

"How do you know this?"

"Because I am here."

What? I didn't have time for this. I turned on my flashlight to figure out where I ended up. This room was filled with golden treasures, lying in layers everywhere on the ground, like some exaggerated adventure film. I couldn't believe it. Browsing through some of the golden piles, I found *it*; *The egg*. A genuine Fabergé egg! *No way!* I had to inspect it multiple times. I ran a finger over the crimson object and felt the texture of the golden ornaments. The colored gems reflected the flashlight, spreading rays of illumination to the surroundings. The room became bright with waving colors, making it feel like I was underwater. Surreal.

"You can keep whatever you find," the orb said.

I smiled. With this egg, I would become famous. I would be the guy who found one of the lost Farbergé eggs. I would finally be a celebrated archeologist. I could take my daughter with me to see the world, explore new artifacts and present her in my press interviews. I could quit that stupid guard job. My life would change forever. I just needed to escape this place first.

The egg was carefully placed in the large inner-pocket of my open jacket. The content of it could be revealed later. With the egg hidden away, the room was now dark again, only with the flashlight illuminating narrow spots of the cave-like walls.

"Look to your left," the orb suggested.

There was nothing but treasures and a monument.

"Pull the arm."

As told, I went to the monument and pulled down the arm of the sitting ape-like figure. A hatch elevated on the wall. For some reason, that didn't surprise me. Traps and secret hatches were part of many stories from the archaeologists at the museum.

As I let go of the hand, the hatch fell again. I stood for a moment, sensing if the sound alerted the creatures, but heard nothing. Then my gaze returned to the hatch. How was I supposed to keep it open? I moved myself there and tried to force it open by hand, but it was too heavy. I browsed through the treasures to see if there was anything useful and ended up with one of the gold plated coconuts. I scratched my head a couple of times. Well, that was worth a try. Returning to the ape's arm, I pulled it down and elevated the hatch. Aiming for the secret opening, I sent the coconut rolling. It went right through, disappearing into the darkness. My bowling skills were not as good as I hoped. I had to try again.

After collecting all the coconuts I could find, I got ready for another attempt. I rolled a coconut, again with too much force, resulting in it disappearing into the dark. The next one had way too little speed and stopped right in front of me. The two next ones came a little closer to the hatch, but not where I wanted them. I felt frustrated. To make things worse, a cry sounded from the passage.

"They are returning," the orb informed. "Hurry up."

I was shaking from stress and anxiety. I tried to roll another coconut. It went right through. Then another. Also right through. This was impossible. An even louder cry sounded, while I had only one coconut left. This was it. I inhaled deeply and prepared the aim. Closing my eyes, I sent the nut rolling. This time, the coconut actually stopped right under the hatch. *I did it!* The coconut would keep the hatch open for me to pass through! I let go of the arm, but as I did, the hatch slammed down and smashed the coconut in a thousand pieces. *Come on!* Two howling cries sounded. The creatures were close.

"Weight," the orb whispered. "Use weight."

Of course! Why didn't I think of that? With feverish haste, I searched the treasures and found a bunch of heavy amulets and diamond filled necklaces before placing them around the hand of the monument. The hatch hovered, yet not enough for me to pass through. I returned to the piles of treasures and threw unuseful objects to the side. The cries intensified and sprinting hooves sounded as they were right beside me, while I heard amulets drop from the monument arm. My sweaty palms almost couldn't grab a hold of the heavy bracelet that finally came to my rescue. Swiftly, I moved to the arm, replaced the dropped amulets and placed the bracelet as well. The weight was just enough to pull the arm down and keep the hatch elevated. As another cry sounded right behind me, I sprinted to the hatch and jumped through the opening, landing like a bunch of dead meat. I heard the amulets and bracelet drop to the floor, and the hatch dropped with an explosive sound, leaving only reverberated silence. I'm not certain, but I might have managed to thank the orb before passing out.

dream

I opened my eyes on the couch in our living room. The TV was still running, but my show was over. I had to stop wasting my time on the couch when I got home from work.

Taking a look out the window, I saw that the sun was shining bright. Perfect. Violet would be home any time soon, and we would head for our usual spot. Tuesday was the best day of the week. This was the day where Mona was out drawing with her croquis friends, leaving Violet and me to have a full evening together. I had Violet all by myself.

"Hey, Dad!" she shouted as she entered the door.

She ran right into my arms for a good, old Tuesday-hug.

"Hi, little jellyfish," I laughed. "How was your day?"

"It was great, Dad. I will tell you on the way. Now, can we go?"

I loved how eager she was. She was looking forward to these Tuesdays just as much as I was. Well, *almost* as much as I was.

"Go get your pack in your room. I'll grab the stuff from the kitchen. The car drives in 2 minutes," I suggested.

Without saying anything, she ran to her room while I went to the kitchen. I packed the usual kitchen gear and food products, and grabbed the surprise right before I left the kitchen. I made sure to hide it well under the box with dough. Violet should better not find it before I gave it to her later that evening.

"I'm ready, Dad!" she informed as I reached the car.

She was fast; Something she had from her mother. I was the slow one in the family, in literally everything. Right now, that didn't concern me, though. It was Tuesday, and I was going to the woods with Violet.

The forest was only a twenty-minute drive from our house. On the way, Violet told me everything about her day at school. She and Emily, her best friends since kindergarten, destroyed one of the braindead mocker-boys. Revenge is rarely ideal, but sometimes it just is. This guy made two girls leave the school by mocking them every day for a whole year, without anybody standing up - until now. Violet and Emily taunted the crap out of him. He cried. I laughed. At that moment, sitting in the car with Violet, I felt complete.

We parked on the side of the road and picked up our gear. The sun delivered some incredible lines of bright light through the trees as we walked on the wide forest path. Of course, the birds were twittering like in fairy tales. Violet and I sang our usual add-on song, where we would add a new word, or sentence, every Tuesday while remembering all the previous words and sentences. We were pretty good, if I should say so, now adding sentence number 42.

"...in a tree - on a branch - with a feather - perfect weather - and a bird - in a nest - with four chicks - eating ticks - having fun..."

We stopped singing as this was where we needed to add a sentence. Violet was quick this time.

"...with a Christmas bun!"

We laughed.

"Well, you are the boss," I informed. *"With a Christmas bun,* it is. Let's remember that next Tuesday."

We continued walking for another ten minutes before reaching our spot: a secret campsite, deep in the woods, with a small stone-marked fireside for our campfire. When we built the place, we placed logs around the hearth, with different heights - some as tables and some as chairs. The site was still untouched by anyone else but us. It was our secret, little place. When we occasionally visited the site on the weekends, we set up a tent and made up scary stories before hiding in our sleeping bags. Sometimes we invited Mona, but she was not as much an outdoor person as we were. She *did* join us from time to time, though.

"Can I light the fire?" Violet asked after we collected some firewood and prepared the campfire.

"Sure thing. Did you remember your fireplow?"

"Oh no! I forgot to bring that. But I have my firestriker."

She took the two little, metallic sticks and stroked them together a few times, generating a rain of crisp sparkles. The woolen tinder ignited perfectly. She blew some air, so the ember from the tinder spread to the kindling with ease, starting the sweet, little campfire. She was becoming good at this. I was so proud. So proud that my eyes got watery.

We spent hours talking and cooking food on the fire, with occasional exploring of the surroundings for more firewood. At one point, a herd of deer sneaked past us, inspecting us, being just as curious as we were. The moment of silence was magical. Violet said she could feel them communicating with us. They wanted to be our friends. I agreed. We were now officially part of the woods, which reminded me of my surprise.

"I got something for you," I said while picking up the gift from my daypack.

Violet took the gift and sent me an inspecting stare. Mona once told me to stop buying things for Violet, when I developed this problem of spoiling her more than once a week. Since then, I had been more modest with the amount of gifts I handed out to her. Violet liked that better as well, I found.

"No way!" she exclaimed after unwrapping the surprise. "How did you get that?"

"I have my methods," I replied with a wink.

I wasn't going to tell her that I *might* have abused my position as a security guard.

"Thanks, Dad. I love it!"

I knew she did. Every time I took her to the museum, she stared at this necklace, hanging on a female mannequin dressed with ancient findings. The leather string was dyed violet and had a vibrant violet attachment curved as a tree. Believe it or not, Violet's favorite color was indeed violet. This ancient necklace was unique, and elegant, so there would be no way to pay for it with money. The last time I saw Violet in love with it, I decided that she would appreciate it more than all of the guests who would ever enter the museum, just roaming blindly, being overwhelmed by all the different objects. The staff would hopefully not notice either.

"I will wear it only when we're alone," Violet informed after putting the necklace around her neck.

I sent her a smile. She was way too smart for a kid in her age. A gorgeous grin was returned to me.

"Hey, are you ready for some *snobrød*?" I asked.

I was becoming good at pronouncing that; *Snobrød* - dough curled around a stick, baked over the fire and filled with jam when baked. Something I learned from my two weeks in Denmark back when I was young. Sometimes I dreamt about those days on the European trip with my friends, missing the feeling of being free and having the world open. I hadn't been out of Canada since then, as Violet came to the world. I wouldn't trade her for anything in the whole universe, though. Nothing could ever take her away from me. She was the love of my life.

"Dad, why are you crying?" she asked.

"I'm just happy, little starfish," I chuckled. "I'm just happy."

The Mind of a Child

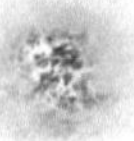

Like every other Monday, Violet sat on her floor, drawing in her room. She was humming happy songs, knowing that tomorrow was Tuesday - her favorite day. Today she drew a boat sailing on the far, blue ocean, with dolphins dancing in the air. Violet had received her mother's creativity, which meant that the other kids in her class often envied her drawing skills. Violet didn't care much about that. She just wanted to dream herself away, living inside of her drawings while creating them.

As she added the final blue stroke to the ocean, she took one last look and placed it in the stack of blue drawings. Content, she exhaled, letting herself find her way back to reality. She looked around her room, absorbing every visual detail she could find; The light passing through her blue glass dolphin on the shelf; The fury fabric of the orange seastar pillow on the bed; The shadows created by the small, wooden clownfish hanging from strings in the ceiling. Nobody, including herself, knew where this interest of the sea came from, but Violet was in love.

One night her father asked her what she wanted to be when she grew older. She didn't doubt the question for a second; She wanted to become one of those people who saves fishes; She desired to clean the oceans from pollution; Like the people on television, having the pleasure to dive with the animals they rescue. Her father told her that it was a good idea and that she should go for it. Violet always looked up to her father - he was cool. Her mother was loved with all of her heart. She loved both of them. When she was younger, her father often read her favorite story out loud: the little mermaid. Every time he did, Violet imagined that she was one of the mermaids in the story, and she was certain that mermaids existed in the real oceans as well. Now she wasn't so sure anymore. That was part of growing older. Hopefully, she would never grow from loving the sea.

Chapter 4

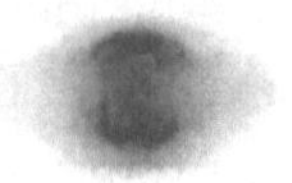

I had seen that before; That stupid monument holding an enormous mirror between its claws. I looked dead in the reflection, with dried blood all over my face. My eyes were encircled by darkness, and my skin was pale as ice. I didn't dare to do more than glance at the mirror every time I ended up in this room. This idiotic room!

"This is the third time we're here! Why?" I asked. "Why are you leading me in circles?"

The glow of the orb dimmed.

"Hey!" I yelled while shaking the damned thing. "Wake up!"

"Your movements don't affect me," the orb whispered.

I stopped shaking.

"The creatures are controlling the cave," it continued. "I'm trapped."

"Trapped? What do you mean, trapped?"

"My presence is imprisoned inside this orb," I was informed. "Guiding is difficult in this state."

"In this state? What are you?"

I was surprised by my question. That was the first time I was able to ask questions about the orb.

"It might be possible to guide if I am unlocked," it whispered. "Currently, the powers of the creatures overrule my abilities to guide."

"What are you?" I asked again.

"I am simply here to help you, Christian."

"So help me by answering my question!"

"Such questions can't be answered in this state. If only I could be unlocked, though I could never ask for such favor."

I took a seat in front of the mirror, aiming the flashlight right into it, illuminating my whole body. Looking at myself, I realized how I was alone with only my reflection and that annoying thing. I felt trapped. No matter what I did, I always ended up in this room. The orb wasn't of any help. I stared so long into the mirror that my reflection lay down, closed its eyes and stopped breathing. Time stopped. Sounds couldn't be heard. Light wasn't visible. Energy didn't exist.

I blinked, and the reflection was sitting again, watching me watching it, with the orb in our hands. The orb pulsed a slow, maroon light, which gave me a tickling feeling around my chest - like something was crawling on my body. My eyes opened wide as a stinging pain rushed through my skin. I smashed my hand into my chest and felt something pop and release a sticky substance between my shirt and my skin; The spider! Within seconds, it felt like my skin, or my whole chest, being pulled towards the sting - like a black hole devouring everything around it. Even my lungs had trouble sucking in air. In a panic, I stood up from the ground, but dizziness hit me hard, forcing me to bend down and put a hand to the floor to regain balance. My other hand moved under my shirt in an attempt to remove the sticky spider guts, but it was solid now. Only the shell of the spider hung onto my hand as I pulled it out. The remaining attached legs moved, making me shake off the thing while the shivering sensation of fright overtook my body. My entire body froze while cold drops of sweat dripped from my forehead. Was I dying?

"Bring the remains to your lips," the orb whispered.

"What?"

"The spider. Bring it to your lips."

I wasn't sure why, but I didn't question the suggestion. The dead spider was found easily and placed in my cramping hand. I felt like throwing up, just holding it there.

"Put it in your mouth and swallow," the orb commanded.

"Wh... Why?"

"Just do it."

The cold sweat rained from my head, while the painful, numbing feeling in my chest spread to the rest of my body. I wouldn't survive. I moved to the dead spider to my lips. The first attempt at placing it in my mouth didn't succeed as my fingers stopped right in front of my spread lips and gagging created loud, choking noises. I just couldn't! The second time didn't do it either - same reaction. This was impossible. The third time I actually threw up, only from imagining the feeling of a crawling spider in my throat; The slimy content of the shell sticking to the tube, all the way down my stomach. I threw up again.

"Enough," the orb said. "You tried. That's good."

"Tried?"

"The sting is not deadly. The pain will fade soon."

"Then why should I swallow the spider?" I raged.

"Let's call it a test - which you passed."

I couldn't believe it. *A test?!* What could ever be the reason for such a sick joke?

"Now, we can work together," the orb continued. "Just await the poison to fade."

Confusion hit me yet again. I remembered the orb saying that it was here for me, but why test me then? In any situation, I needed that orb. I had no clue how to escape without it. If the orb was to help me, I just needed to 'unlock' it somehow.

"Very well," I said. "Tell me what to do."
The orb started glowing brightly.

dream

The alarm clock played its horrible beeps a dozen times before I smashed it silent and sneaked out the bedroom door. With my vitamins swallowed, and my brown mug of instant coffee in my hand, I had a sip by the window. The ticking wall clock showed 07.25. Yes, there he was… The idiotic neighbor, jogging with his burning cigarette in his mouth. I often wondered if he ever washed that horrific red suit, with its enormous spots of sweat printed on the back, and under his arms, and between his chubby breasts, all the way down his bouncing beer-belly. How I hated that guy.

"Good morning, Dad!" Violet yawned while the half-past tone played from the clock.

We came home quite late last night, so I didn't blame her for being tired. She hugged me a long morning-hug, reminding me that she didn't shower the smoke from the campfire off last night, simply being too exhausted.

"Remember what you promised me last night, little oyster?" I asked her with a smile.

"Of course, Dad," she replied. "I just wanted to thank you again for the necklace. I love it so much."

I couldn't stop smiling.

"I love you, Violet - you know that, right?"

"Of course, Dad. I love you too."

She ran for her shower while Mona came down the stairs

and went to the kitchen. I looked out the window again while enjoying the rest of my coffee. The air contained a strange kind of fog, but nothing of concern. The sun was shining bright on the horizon, looking somewhat idyllic with the clear lines of sunlight penetrating the blurring fog. Maybe this day would be good, I thought. Perhaps something new and exciting would happen. I often felt this on Wednesday mornings, when still high on Tuesday nights. The days always turned out to be the same, though; Boring and mostly meaningless. Nevertheless, the eight o'clock tone sounded, and I had to leave for work.

"Have fun, Dad!" Violet shouted from the bathroom window as I reached the car.

"Have fun, little goldfish!"

Chapter 5

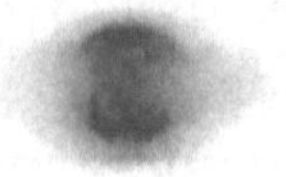

The bony, ape-like creature jumped onto me, forcing the air out of my lungs. Its skin was cold and greasy, and the breaths smelled like decaying fish. The black eyes, with the tiny white pupils, flickered from an intense rage while staring me deep in the eyes. As I was about to pass out, my muscles were forced into a relaxed state, resulting in my body being squeezed out of its disgusting arms. Before the creature could grab me again, I ran. It was following me close, crawling fast in jumping motions. Panic! It grabbed my foot, and my body smashed down the ground, sending a deep pain through my flat palms all the way down my spine. I shouted from fear and agony. The flashlight broke in the fall, now flickering intensely on the ground in front of me. Revolting saliva dripped down my neck. I closed my eyes. Everything became dark - almost black - yet more… violet.

VIOLET!

It couldn't end like this! Violet needed me. I found myself flipping over and kick the ape-like creature, giving me a moment to flee. I found a pile of golden treasures and fiddled my way through to end up with a heavy scepter - similar to a mace. I was prepared for a killing blow. The creature sprinted towards me while I raised my weapon, neglecting the flickering from the flashlight, making the movements in the room appear faster than they were. I wasn't sure how close the creature was when I swung my weapon, yet I hit it with all of my strength. It released a horrifying cry, as it was enraged. I could sense the anger. This wasn't good. As I raised the weapon again, the creature punched it out of my hand, took hold of my feet and lifted me, with my head hanging down. All I could see in the flickering light was the long legs - thin as bone - pale as ash. I felt its grip tighten around my ankles. It was torture. I tried grabbing out for another relic, but I could not reach. The orb fell out of my pocket and hit the ground like a brick from a wall. As the flashlight finally died, all that was left was the dim glow from the orb. I felt a hand searching my body for a soft spot to penetrate my skin and rip out my guts. I imagined the blood running from my stomach, down my face and landing on the ground.

"I'm sorry, Violet," I mumbled as I understood this was the end.

While I began taking my final breaths, I stared at the orb. It was pulsing rapidly, like the heart from a falling climber. The pulsating only increased in speed - until it abruptly died. Everything became dark.

"Sorry for this," it whispered.

A blinding flash appeared for a split-second, and I felt a burning sensation. Blinded, I was thrown to the ground. The smell was the same as when Violet and I burned our chicken-sticks on the campfire; Disgusting. It took a while before my eyes adjusted, being able to see again. The orb still contained a bit of the flash, illuminating the room with beautiful, bright light. Behind me was the remains of the creature, now lying in a pile of bones, with a piece of smoking skin.

"You saved me," I informed the orb, like a confused kid. "This time you actually saved me."

"Don't be so sure yet."

I looked down my shirt and saw large stains of blood. As I

lifted the shirt, I saw a piece of the broken fabergé egg penetrating my stomach. Within seconds, I felt weak. It took a few inhales before I dared to touch the piece and pull it out of my body. I cramped up immediately. The golden and silver grains of sand - the content of the egg - found its way into the open wound, resulting in my crying from agony. I was burning up from the inside, with grains eating me like acid. I felt it hard to breathe as the world began to spin.

"Put me to your wound," the orb whispered.

Yet again, I did as the orb suggested. I had no reason not to. In the worst case, the orb was testing me. I picked it up and placed it on my stomach, lightly touching the wound. The white light turned amber, releasing a warm sensation on my skin. A moment later, it became white again.

"Now, remove me."

I removed the orb and stared at the wound. It was filled with cream-colored liquid, and the pain was not as severe. The orb healed me somehow.

"How can I ever thank you?" I asked, despite already knowing the answer.

There was no reason for me not to trust the orb. It had informed that it was here for me, and now it also proved it; It killed the creature and healed my wound. The hope of getting out of this place alive emerged. I would see Violet again soon. First, there was one thing to do, though. I didn't doubt it for a second.

"I will unlock you. Tell me where to go."

dream

The office clock chimed my eyes open. It was time to get back to work. The door to the neighbor's office was open yet again, and I couldn't resist stopping, listening to the three geeks discuss whatever nerdy subjects they were up to today. Peeking inside, I saw them all standing up, making aggressive arm-movements as the conversation was intense. One of the male geeks talked about some pollution created by *"The Power."*

"We have to do something!" the female geek yelled.

"But we don't have any proof," the other male informed.

"I know," the first male said. "It will be hard to fight, but we will succeed!"

Well, I heard enough. These obscure games weren't of my interest. I had a job to do after all, so I found my way to the lobby. There were no visitors, leaving the area quiet and peaceful. It gave me time to roam while considering what I should buy for Violet's birthdays in a few weeks. How could I beat that necklace? I obviously couldn't take more stuff from the museum. Maybe I could get her something for our Tuesdays. A new knife? Or perhaps it was time for her to receive a hatchet and learn chopping wood. She would love that. I imagined the smile she would have after chopping her first little log. I wished I could see her smile later, but she was having a sleepover at Emily's. It made me sad to think about being home without seeing her. Well, maybe she would call me when I was off work. She did that sometimes, just calling to chat. I hoped she would. I certainly wouldn't disturb her by calling myself. She needed her freedom.

I picked up my phone and found a new message from Mona informing me that she would be home late because of work. With that information received, I fast-dialed the local pizza house.

"Hi, it's Christian... Yes, exactly, the usual. Same time as always."

Chapter 6

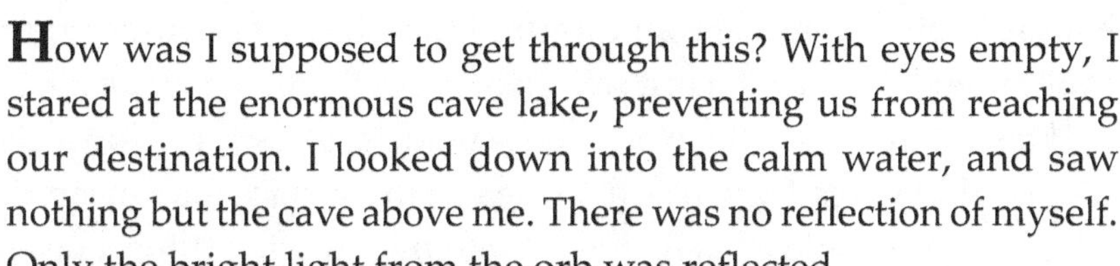

How was I supposed to get through this? With eyes empty, I stared at the enormous cave lake, preventing us from reaching our destination. I looked down into the calm water, and saw nothing but the cave above me. There was no reflection of myself. Only the bright light from the orb was reflected.

"What is this?" I asked.

The orb didn't answer. Instead, it changed into a jet-black sphere, emitting a strange cyan light. I couldn't see the point from which the light was created, but the whole cave was illuminated with this obscure color. Something was swimming in the water, now being fully visible, glowing slightly from the reflection of the light. It reminded me of thin piranhas with their skull-like faces, dead eyes and needle teeth.

Bending down, I put my hand in the cold water. Instantly the lake creatures accelerated towards my hand, and as they neared, I felt some kind of electricity and pulled my hand up in a panic.

"You should avoid those," the orb whispered.

"Can you help?" I asked, in the hope that the orb could just vaporize them or the like.

"Unfortunately, I lost most of my power in destroying the creature earlier," it replied. "I will need time to regenerate. Time we don't have."

I watched the creatures for a while. They were everywhere, floating silently in the water, only occasionally racing towards random locations before continuing their roaming. There was no way to cross the lake without getting attacked. I examined the cave with all of its strange roots hanging down from the ceiling. At one point, I saw a drop of water drip from one of them into the lake, resulting in racing of the creatures towards the rings created on the water surface. I realized that the creatures had no eyes in their eye sockets, and figured that they were attracted to motion in the water. To test my theory, I gathered a few artifacts and tossed them into the water. The creatures were lured towards the spot but spread again as the rings on the surface disappeared. What to do? I couldn't keep them lured by throwing things. I was about to ask the orb for guidance before my eyes found a possible solution. Moving to the object, I picked it up; A golden hourglass with silvery sand. I turned it upside down and inspected the sparkling grains that filled the bottom. The hourglass was slow, but I couldn't measure how long it took for it to finish. It was a long shot, but I had nothing else to do, so I removed the golden top and broke a hole in the glass. I removed my shoes and jacket, ready for a cold swim. Before entering the water, I grabbed one of the long roots hovering above the water surface. I attached the hourglass, upside down, to let the silver grains drip into the water, creating a stream of motion rings on the surface. The creatures gathered around the grains. It was working! I had to move!

"Holy hell!" I cried as my body hit the freezing water.

Luckily, the creatures weren't capable of hearing. I moved through the water, fluent as liquid from a winter-nose. As hoped, the creatures were busy inspecting the grains from my trap. However, as I looked back, I saw that the hourglass emptied quicker than expected. It only had half of the grains left - and I still needed two-thirds of the way.

"Holy bloody hell!" I heard my trembling voice yell again,

knowing how idiotic that sounded.

I speeded up, despite knowing that it would create more motion through the water, and I already felt the electricity from one of the bloody creatures behind me. I was hunted. The thing was rapid and found its way in front of me. It snapped my hand, allowing me to explore its hundreds of tiny teeth, sending a shockwave through my whole body. I managed to hold onto the orb in my hand, but I felt the blood flowing from my wounds. The creature prepared to attack again, but this time the orb flashed and the dead creature disappeared into the lake bottom.

"Quick!" it whispered.

I glanced back and saw the last grain of sand leave the hourglass.

"Holy damned bloody hell!" My voice exploded.

I swam the fastest I could. I saw the edge right there in front of me, yet I didn't see it coming closer as I raced towards it. I felt the electricity from all of the creatures rushing towards me. My body tightened and cramped up from the shock level. I felt a bite in my arm and blood escaped. I felt another bite in my wrist and even more blood escaped. I felt a bite around two of my fingers, and I heard the snappy sound as they were pulled off my hand, by the strength of the creature's tiny teeth. The pain was overwhelming. This time, I was convinced that I wouldn't make it. My whole body was tickling from being electrified and eaten alive. Blood was floating everywhere, while my heart kept racing, emptying my veins into the water. The loud splashes, created by my panicky arm-paddling, blinded my vision. I couldn't stand it any longer. I cried as I found solid ground and dragged my bleeding body up the shore. My eyes closed. Only time would reveal if I made it or not.

dream

An explosion sounded, making me jump up from the couch. I had been lying on the remote, accidentally keeping the volume button pressed, but found the remote and fumbled the volume down to a tolerable level. Sitting on the couch, rubbing my face, I heard Mona enter from the front door.

"Hi, darling," she greeted and kissed me on the cheek. "Pizza again, huh?

"How was work?" I asked.

"Was fine. How was your day?"

"Same as always."

"That's excellent, dear."

She looked exhausted. She had been working overtime a lot lately, pressured by her new boss. She liked her job, so she wasn't complaining. However, it surely wasn't healthy working that much.

"Can I get you something?" I asked, feeling like doing something kind for my wife.

"Thank you, love. I will just shower and head to bed. We have a long presentation at work tomorrow, so I need my mind fresh."

She kissed me on my head and stroked my shoulder tattoo before heading upstairs.

"I love you!" she yelled from the stairway.

"Love you too!"

The touch of her hand gave me goosebumps, and I had to

scratch the area to make it go away. I couldn't help it as I studied the teddy bear tattoo I was condemned to wear for the rest of my life. Thinking back on the time when I got it was painful. I didn't feel like that guy anymore, despite how much I missed being him. I didn't like who I had become. Mona always loved the teddy, though, and so did Violet. When I considered having it removed, they raised objections; *"We stand up, for teddy bear rights!"* they shouted, managing to create so much positivity suppressing the negative. A smile formed on my face. If only every day could be days like that.

I trashed the greasy pizza box and went to the cupboard, where I found my hidden bottle of Scotch. After pouring up half a glass, I hid the bottle again and moved to the window. I looked at the stars. I sipped. I looked at the moon. Another sip. I looked at the haze under the functioning streetlight at the end of the street. Another sip. I wondered what Violet was doing at this moment, while I sipped again. Maybe I should get her name engraved in that hatchet. She would love that! Another sip. And another sip. And anoth…

The glass was empty already. There was no point in staying up any longer, so I found my way upstairs to lie down next to a snoring Mona. She didn't wear those nasal dilators we got her last month, so I plugged my ears instead. I wanted to put my arm around her, but the fear of awaking her overruled. Instead, I just lay on my back, staring up into the darkness.

The World of Mona

Mona entered the bathroom and closed the door, keeping it unlocked, just in case. She slipped off her clothes, turned on the water and waited for the steam to appear. She liked her showers boiling hot.

Placing herself under the rain of pleasure, she exhaled, feeling the fatigue arrive. Another day of hard work was over, but with great results. The new boss would love the pitch Mona and her colleague made ready to present the next day. Her career as an art director would finally take off, and even though her work was for TV advertising, and not movies, the hard work was kind of fun - for now. She was doing something she liked, hopefully turning it into a job she would *love*.

A sound pulled her out of her thoughts. She hoped it was Christian entering as she glanced out the shower curtain, but it wasn't. There was no one there. She heard another sound and recognized that it was a liquor bottle. Christian was drinking from his "secret" whiskey again.

Filled with guilt, Mona started shampooing her hair. She knew that it wasn't her fault, but she should be there for him. She felt terrible that Christian never got to fulfill his dreams of archeology. She had to speak to him about it; Tell him to read those books and go outside digging or whatever. Just do *something*. Find a hobby. Pull himself together!

She exhaled again, filled with even more guilt. The fatigue had taken over. She wanted to take it all back, knowing that Christian worked the guard job to give Violet a stable childhood. He was the best father in the world. Such a good man. One day, when her work would allow her, she would spend more time with him. After all, he was the love of her life, and always would be.

Chapter 7

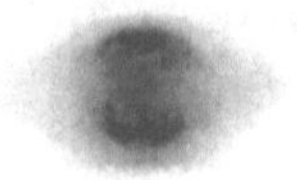

I stared like a mad man. For ages. Just staring and staring at the orb on the ground in front of me. My eyes were dry from staring. I stared at the mesmerizing lights it emitted. The shifting of colors from maroon to orange to purple and back, with sparkling golden particles that occasionally morphed into a golden ball before breaking into tiny particles again. It continued like this for hours, while I was just staring. The bleeding from my wounds had stopped a long time ago, and the pain from my lost fingers had eased. I assumed the orb had something to do with that. That god damned orb.

"I'm sorry," it whispered while continuing the alluring motions.

"Sorry for what?" I asked, still staring.

"Everything."

"Everything?"

"Your life."

"My life? Am I dead?"

"No, you are still alive."

"Then I don't understand."

The orb became quiet for a while, but I was used to that now.

"Thank you," it whispered.

"What for?"

"For being alive."

First now I understood. The orb needed me just as much as I

needed it. It had no power without me - and it was all I knew after waking up in this place. I was used to its presence, and probably wouldn't survive without it.

Finally, I was able to remove my eyes and get up from the ground. I tried to pick up the orb but dropped it again through my missing fingers. I inspected the bone sticking out one of them, amazed by how calm I was. There were more important things in the world than those two fingers.

"I can fix you, friend," the orb informed. "When I'm unlocked, your life won't be the same."

I smiled and picked up the orb with my other hand.

"Thank you, friend," I said.

Then something caught my attention; Two green luminous dots were moving on my shoulder. I narrowed my eyes and noticed the dots to be the eyes of my bear tattoo. It was animated, turning its head from side to side, flapping the arms up and down. Watching a tattoo come to life, dancing on my shoulder like that, should naturally freak me out, but whatever force kept me calm, did it well.

"Are you doing this?" I asked the orb.

Instead of replying, the orb turned white and shined bright, illuminating the space around us, revealing a large marble double-door next to us. I knew exactly what was behind that door.

dream

I checked my alarm clock from the bed. Still five minutes before it started beeping. That never happened before. I decided to cancel the alarm, sneak out of the room and do my morning routine five minutes early. Standing by the window, with my coffee, I waited for the wall clock to show 07.25. When it did, I stared out the window, awaiting the annoying neighbor to jog by. He was never late.

"That's strange," I mumbled, sipping from my mug.

The clock played its half-past tone, and a smile was forming on my face, but disappeared when I remembered that Violet was at Emily's. I stared out the window again, watching the strange fog flow by. It reminded me of the smoke from the neighbor's annoying cigarettes. I waited five more minutes before deciding that he wasn't jogging today. It felt wrong.

Emptying my mug, I realized that I forgot to take my vitamins; That wouldn't be good. I moved to the kitchen, found the pills and swallowed them dry, as usual. This time they felt stuck in my throat, and I had to drink a glass of water to release them. The bitter taste was glued to my tongue for the rest of the day. I even filled a new mug of coffee, with two spoons of sugar, in a desperate attempt to remove the taste.

"Morning, my love," Mona said as she came down the stairs, already dressed for work.

She gave me a genuine kiss. A long one. I couldn't remember

when was the last time she gave me one of those; The soft kisses that made me fall in love with her over and over. I was out of words as she ended the kiss, took a sip of my coffee and rushed out the door. She had that important presentation at work. Sitting there in her car, she looked fresh and ready, blowing me a kiss before driving away. A kiss that I caught and put in my pocket, just as when we were young.

"What the…"

Chapter 8

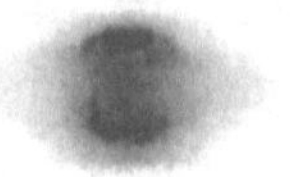

The marble double-door was twice the height of myself, with carvings of various beings looking at each other. Above each being was carved an hourglass. As there was no indication of handles, I found my way to the door to inspect it further. I touched it with the tip of my finger and instantly felt a tickling sensation on my chest. As a reflection, I jumped backward, almost tripping over my own feet. I couldn't believe it. I tried touching the door again and felt the same touch on my chest. I ran my fingers from the top of the door and downwards, and felt the tickling touch running down my forehead, nose and mouth. I removed my hand. The door was connected to me somehow. But how? Would it kill me if I attempted to break it? In curiosity, I punched the door with a heavy blow and the pain hit me hard, both in my hand and in my chest. I tried kicking the door near the ground and felt the blow on my shin. Everything about this felt wrong. I dared to try and push the door open, but only felt the force reflect on my body - the door itself didn't move.

"Any suggestions?" I asked the orb.

As it stayed quiet, I sat down in front of the door to consider my options. I was freezing and felt sick. The chilly water from the lake had given me a cold and I felt another sneeze building up. I didn't have time to prepare myself before the sneeze erupted and sent a shot of human fluids out the air. Getting myself back up from the sneeze, I was surprised to see that some of the door had dissolved where the fluids hit.

"Sometimes the natural rules the unnatural," the orb whispered.

Right. I touched some of the dissolved areas and concluded that they were indeed tiny holes and not just an illusion. The feeling of having ants running under my skin arrived, so I removed my finger again. An idea popped into my head. I searched the treasures around me and ended up with what I assumed was a small, golden singing bowl. Not the best tool, but better than my hands. The bowl was filled by dipping it in the water, before being moved to the door and splashed out, creating a hand-sized hole in the door. I peeked through but couldn't see much; It was total darkness in there. The smell reminded me of a hot sauna filled with bloaty men. It wasn't inviting, so to say - but I had to get it there. I scooped up more water and splashed it at the door and repeated the procedure until there was a hole large enough to pass through. I stared at the dissolved door for a while.

"What happens when I pass?" I asked.

"You become a hero," the orb whispered.

Even though my question was concerning pain, or even death, I accepted the reply. The door was beginning to repair itself, so I had to act swiftly. Closing my eyes and inhaling, I put a foot through the hole. The tickling sensation of having ghosts stepping through my body gave me goosebumps, and in an awkward maneuver, I threw myself through the hole. As I lay on the other side, I started laughing from the tickling sensation all over my body. I just couldn't stop. The volume was intense. Was that actually me releasing this noise? I almost couldn't breathe from laughing. I panicked. My body cramped up while my loud voice cried out its fake happiness. Was I dying? Was it even possible to die from laughter? I couldn't think clearly as my vision began to generate colored spots everywhere I looked. I was terrified, yet I continued laughing out loud, curled up on the ground like a child having a ball shot at its belly. My fingers and toes turned numb. The blood in my veins wasn't moving. The painful numbness spread to my hands and feet, all the way up to my forehead. I felt my body giving up, joint by joint. Within moments, the numbness had spread to most of my body. It was torture.

"Await the door," the orb whispered.

I managed to turn my head and saw that the hole was nearly filled again. I just had to wait it out - give it time - although time felt infinite at that point. I wasn't able to consider what would happen when the door was repaired. The colored spots in my vision were slowly defeated by black areas, making me blind little by little. I couldn't handle the cramping laughing anymore. It had to stop - *now!*

"The door is almost complete," I was informed. "Synchronize. Now!"

Closing my eyes, I visualized the hole closing. I couldn't think of anything else. The same image played over and over of the completion of the door. Every time it closed, a new layer was added. It became harder. Unbreakable.

Suddenly my eyes, mouth and nostrils were forced wide open. My laughter stopped, while my body was stretching long on the ground, as if something was pulling me in each end. I felt my bones being torn apart by my own strength. Everything felt wrong. The numbness felt like I was stroked by hundreds of whips, slashing with electric power - and I couldn't do anything to stop it.

"Give in," I heard the whisper say. "Trust me."

I didn't need the orb to tell me that - I was ready, once again, to surrender. This agony wasn't worth it.

A bright star showed itself in the distance, eliminating my visualizations of the repairing door. The glare was incredible - a million vibrant colors taking over my vision, while I felt a warm blanket wrapping around my cramping body. I felt relaxed, despite not being able to move. I didn't want it to end.

"You did good," it whispered. "I'm proud of you."

dream

My head dropped from my hand as my phone vibrated on the table next to my elbow. It wasn't the alarm telling me that the break was over - it was a call from Mona. That was strange. She never called me at work.

"It's Christian," I mumbled after putting the phone to my ear.

I could hear that she was sitting in her car with that horrible, noisy engine and the usual road ambiance. She breathed heavily into the phone.

"Christian," she said - I think. "Something happened."

The car noise made it difficult to hear her speaking.

"What happened, Mona?"

"It's Violet…"

Her voice disappeared in the noise.

"Mona?"

The call was disconnected. I felt my heart rate increase. *What happened to Violet?* The stressful tone from Mona made me sweat. *Did something serious happen?* I called Mona's phone and listened to the calling beeps - but the call was cut off. *What the hell?* I called again and the same thing happened. Then I texted Mona to call me. The situation made me stand up and walk in circles, just awaiting her call. I wasn't sure why, but I was convinced that something horrible had happened - even though it might just be that Violet was sent home after taking down that bullying jerk - or something mild like that.

Suddenly I heard something crack under my foot.

"Goddammit!"

My glasses were broken; Completely destroyed by my stupidly huge security shoe. I swept them up from the ground and tossed them into the trash bin. This was the third pair broken this month. There was only one pair left in my stash of cheap plastic glasses, and they were hideous. I was tired of being this clumsy; Nothing but a gigantic idiot! What the hell was wrong with me?

Finally, the phone vibrated again.

"Mona! What's happening?" I exclaimed.

This time the car noise was gone. Mona was running.

"Come to the hospital *now!* Violet is in a coma!"

The blood disappeared from my head. The world was spinning while my mouth dried up like a bag of flour.

"What? How? Why?" I stuttered.

I could hear her ask a nurse for direction to the room in which Violet was. Mona almost couldn't speak between the exhausting breaths.

"Violet and Emily… They collapsed on their way to school… Both in a coma… Don't know more yet… Christian, come!"

"I'm on my way!"

I picked up my keys and ran to the door before pulling it open and sprinting right into one of the geeks who just left their office. We stopped and watched each other. He looked suspicious, but I didn't have time. I ran before he managed to open his mouth.

Chapter 9

No! No! No! How could I forget? My daughter was sick. Why the hell was I not with her? She needed me!

"How far are we from leaving this place?" I asked.

"Not far," the bright orb replied.

Desperation. I had no control over this. Why did I leave my daughter in the first place? What in the world could be *that* important? Gold? Treasures?

"I need to get out," I commanded.

"We're close."

"Where do I go?"

"One moment."

I waited. Patiently.

"So?" I asked eagerly after the moment had passed.

The orb was quiet.

"Wake up!" I yelled and shook the damned thing in the air.

Still no response. I didn't have time for this! The impatience brought back the stressful tickling in my body. I didn't know whether to cry or laugh, but I was furious.

"Wake the hell up!" I yelled.

The rage took control of me and I tossed the orb hard on the ground. In an instance, the bright light disappeared and everything became dark.

"Don't play this game with me!" I cried.

I fumbled around in the darkness to find the orb. But it was gone. I was lost in this empty space - trapped - with a painful urge to see my daughter again. Desperation took me this time, and I started crawling, searching for the thing. How would I get out without it? What was I thinking? My speed increased every second.

"I'm sorry!" I exclaimed. "Show me where you are, please."

A deep neigh-like sound echoed around me. A creature was coming.

"Please," I cried.

The orb created a quick flash in the distance. How did I end up so far from it? I tried memorizing where the flash was created and ran towards the point, but miscalculated the distance and ended up stepping on the thing instead. I fell - my head hitting the ground hard. Agony. Tears. Again, my eyes were forced closed.

Childhood Memories

Christian became six years old that day. His father had promised to take him to the woods to dig for treasures, why Christian jocked home instead of walking. He just couldn't wait.

A few weeks ago, the television had broadcasted a documentary about the discovery of artifacts for the new museum in town. Ever since seeing that, Christian knew that he wanted to be an archeologist.

His father was a good man. However, good men aren't perfect - Christian learned that on this day. When he finally arrived home from school, his father wasn't in the house. Christian waited for two hours before their landline phone rang in the living room. It was his father calling to say happy birthday; He wouldn't be home before late, as something important happened at work. Christian was broken. Within minutes, he was furious and kicked the front door open. The tools for digging were in the shed, where small boys weren't allowed, but he didn't care about that. He kicked the shed door open and grabbed a hand-sized spade and a shovel before heading out the woods.

The weather was cloudy and grey, yet the birds were twittering. Christian dug a hundred holes, but found nothing of interest. No matter how much he dug, his anger was still raging. How should he ever find a treasure without his father? What was so important at work? Christian roared from his fury and threw the tools as long as he could. Tears formed in his eyes, he thought, but that turned out to be incoming rain.

He sought shelter from the rain in the entrance of a vault. To his surprise, the vault door was open this time. It had never been before, so Christian became curious and went inside. The space was dark and cold, and it only took a couple of steps for the poor boy to fall down a three-meter drop. The door was shut by the wind, leaving Christian terrified in the dark. He had no idea where he was or how he would get out. He tried calling for help, but who would hear him? He missed his father. What if he never saw him again. What if he was stuck here forever?

The frightened birthday-boy tried in blind to find a way out, taking one step at a time, following the cold rock walls with his right hand. His father once told him, that if trapped in a maze, doing this would eventually lead to the exit. What Christian didn't think of was that such a technique doesn't work when the exit is above.

Something was awakening in the ceiling. What kind of monster would live in such a place? Christian's heart raced as he sat down and held his breath. The monster was flapping its wings like crazy. *It must be searching for me*, the little boy thought. He sat there, awaiting his death, for who knows how long. Just until a bright flash blinded him from above; His father had found him.

A lot of tears were shared between Christian and his father that night. The father had never been so scared in his life. He had developed a bad conscience from not being with his son on his birthday, so he told his boss to go to hell, before he went home to the empty house. He couldn't live with himself if anything happened to his boy. He searched the woods for hours. It was a desperate long-shot to check the vault door, as it hadn't been open for ages. Seeing his son sitting crumbled up like that was an eye-opener. From that day, he made sure to spend at least one day a week with his boy, searching for treasures in the woods, with their new dog. They never discovered any treasures, but he loved spending the time there, just as much as Christian did. Christian couldn't wish for a better father.

dream

"Excuse me," the nurse apologized. "I have news."

Lifting my head from the hospital bed, I checked to see if Violet was awake before I moved my attention to the nurse.

"No, please, remain seated," she suggested.

"Bad news?"

"Well…"

She paused while the lump in my throat grew to a choking size.

"…both good and bad."

"What does that mean?"

I moved my gaze to Violet again. She looked calm, just sleeping silently. It was beyond my grasp that she was sick. My little girl. What was wrong?

"Have you watched the news, Christian?"

"The news?"

"Children are getting sick all over town. Apparently, it's a local disease resulting in infection of vital parts of the brain and nervous system. The origins are still unknown as the disease has only recently been discovered…"

The information made me pull my hands to my head, resulting in a glass of water being pushed to the floor, splintering in a thousand pieces. The loud, reverbing sound muted the nurse.

"Are you telling me that there's no cure?" I asked.

She studied me for a while.

"There is no cure yet, no."

My eyes closed.

"However," she continued. "There is a treatment that will let your daughter live as normal until a cure is discovered."

The feet of my chair generated a loud scratching sound as I stood up.

"She needs that treatment!" I exclaimed with hope growing inside me.

The nurse looked to the ground while moving her arm out. There was a document in her hand.

"These are the bad news," she said.

I stared at her, awaiting eye-contact. I needed her eyes to tell me how bad the news was, before I read them. She restrained to let that happen, so I eventually took the document from her hand.

"I'm sorry, Christian," she said before leaving the room.

I picked up my cell phone and found Mona's number, as I couldn't bear to read the news alone. However, something prevented me from pressing the call button. Maybe the thought of awakening Mona, if the news wasn't actually *that* bad. Mona hadn't slept since arriving at the hospital yesterday afternoon, and her crying left her eyes dark and broken. In the end, I insisted that she went home while I stayed watching our daughter. She needed a proper sleep not to go insane.

I started reading the document. It was a lot of information about the benefits of keeping the patient alive, though also a long list of possible side-effects. It was noted multiple times that these side-effects were never recorded, as the treatment hadn't had time to be tested. Everything I read seemed perfect - until I got to the bottom; The price. It wasn't correct. It had to be a mistake. The production couldn't be *that* expensive - could it? I checked the back of the document, feeling that there had to be more information about the price. I moved my fingers over the price-notes while reading them to myself once more. There were three different prices: one for the first month, one for the second month, and one for the remaining time. The second month was half the cost of the first, while the remaining months were half the price of the second month. The first payment was insane, but necessary as the treatment was more intense in the beginning.

How the hell were we going to pay for this? I wanted to speak to the nurse again, though I wasn't sure why. Maybe I just wanted to complain and release some of my growing anger. As I took the first step towards the door, something dropped from my pocket; The necklace I gave Violet last Tuesday. I picked it up and studied it while a tear escaped my eye. Why did I even consider this?

Picking up the phone, I called Mona.

"Contact the bank. Call the real estate agent. Start selling everything we own. We need money."

Chapter 10

Everything was black as I got up from the fall. The deep pain in the back of my head hit me hard as the blood returned to my head. I felt dizzy, yet I couldn't see if the world was actually spinning. Something in the dark called out for me. I fiddled to find the orb, but it wasn't there.

Before I managed to take any other action, a quick flash appeared from around the corner, and a beast-like cry sounded but died just as fast. A pulsing, purple light initiated, luring me to glance around the corner. The orb was lying in the claws of smoking remains of a creature appearing once to be some enormous cat. I picked up the pulsing orb, which again contained golden particles floating in the purple light.

"What happened?" I asked.

"What do you mean?"

"Why did the creature settle with taking you? Why spare my life?"

"Why do you ask?"

"I ask because I want answers to my questions."

The orb laughed.

"It comforts me that you ask such questions. Just as much as you will enjoy hearing the answer."

I had no idea what that meant.

"These creatures," the orb continued. "They wish to exploit my powers. You are worth nothing to them, while I am worth everything. All they want is me."

The logic in what was said made me trust in the words.

"Your best option is to unlock me, friend. When not imprisoned, I am capable of destroying every single creature we may stumble upon on our way out."

"I was going to do that," I said.

"I know, friend."

All of a sudden, I sensed eyes watching me from the dark space around us. The hairs on my body raised. I knew that the orb didn't have the strength to illuminate the area yet, so I grabbed and moved it around in the air with purpose. I wasn't sure why, but I hoped to see the dim, purple light reflect in the eyes of the watching creatures. Maybe *knowing* that they were there wasn't as scary as *sensing* their presence. I didn't spot any reflections, yet I saw a mark on the ground from where I awoke. An arrow scratched in the rock, pointing in the opposite direction of where the creature was headed.

"Just around the corner." the orb whispered before I could make any sense of the situation.

I turned around and saw a dusky light from the passage for which the creature was headed. The mechanism was close. It wouldn't be long before I escaped and hugged my beautiful daughter again.

dream

I jumped up from the couch as my phone rang on the floor. I must have dropped it while closing my eyes. Picking it up, I noted that the call was from the real estate agent. My voice was quivering as I took the call.

Only a few minutes passed before the conversation ended and I put down the phone again. I couldn't believe it. That was the best news I had heard for years; The news I had been waiting for since contacting the agent for an express sale of the house, with a ridiculously low price. The house was sold, and the buyer had accepted the condition of an instant payment. It only took four days to sell the house, thanks to that painful deal, but we didn't have any more time to waste. Now we had money to pay for the first treatment - and even money the second month - and almost for a whole year.

I drove as fast as I could to the hospital. I didn't even have time to call Mona to tell her the great news. She could have them when I arrived, as she was already there. The sun was shining bright, illuminating every tree, bush and flower on the way. I might have run a red light or two, but the joy inside of me made sure I continued with full speed. It didn't take me long to reach the hospital, find a parking spot and run towards the nurse's office. I realized how vibrant the colors were on the hospital walls; Some red, some green, some yellow, and even some Violet. It felt like I was running inside a rainbow. This place wasn't that bad after all.

"Jenny!" I yelled as I saw the nurse having lunch in her colorful office. "I have good news!"

She stood up as she saw me running inside with a grin on my face.

"We have money! We can save Violet!"

A smile appeared on her face. I hadn't seen her smile like that before; A nervous smile. It was like time stopped as a tear ran down her chin, past her curving mouth before falling to the ground. In the silence, I could hear the drop explode on the floor. She didn't move. She didn't say anything. She just stood there with her silly smile printed on her soft face, staring at my shirt.

"Jenny?" my voice trembled. "Is everything alright?"

No reaction. In an instant, all the vibrant colors blended to grey. The lifeless office darkened as a thick cloud covered the sun outside the window, while the air became cold, giving me chills from my neck down my spine. The world disappeared for a second.

"Jenny?"

She looked up. For the first time in my life, I saw pure terror in another person's eyes. A terror that continued devouring me ever since I heard the words from her silent mouth.

"I… I have bad news."

Chapter 11

I roared.

My voice reverberated into the darkness. It couldn't be true! Violet wasn't dead! I wouldn't believe it! However, the dream felt very real - and deep inside, I knew it was indeed true. My daughter wasn't there when I got out. I would never see her again - never hug her - never enjoy our Tuesdays in the woods. My little dolphin. My seastar.

I sobbed.

The thought was overwhelming. Once more, I smashed the orb hard down the ground and let my foot fly through a bunch of golden artifacts. I couldn't control myself. My anger exploded. I yelled - and cried - and wailed, my fists clenched with full strength; The feeling of having my heart sucked out of my chest; The painful tickling deep inside my stomach; The uncertainty of what to do with myself. I kept raging until my body didn't contain any more energy, and I had to sit down with the remaining tears escaping my eyes. The space became quiet.

"I just needed more time," I heard myself mumble.

"I can help you, friend."

The color of the orb flared with divine yellow light.

"How can you help me? My daughter is dead!"

"You said you needed more time."

"Can you give me more time?"

"Well, I am the opposite of time."

"Why do you speak in riddles?!"

"I don't, friend."

I was furious. I was tired of being loaded with vague answers from the orb, yet I had become attached to the damned thing. It was my friend. It supported me all this way, and I couldn't blame it for speaking the way it did. You can not change the language of another being. Things are as they are. So I ended up apologizing.

"When I am unlocked, I will fix your sorrows," the orb whispered. "I will fix the world."

"So, I will have more time with my daughter?"

"That will never be a problem again. Don't worry. I will help you. Friend."

dream

I lifted my head from the hospital bed. Violet was lying lifeless, pale as never before. She didn't breathe. She didn't move. She didn't live. I had no more tears left in my body, yet my dry eyes attempted to cry. Mona was sitting on the other side of the bed, staring at Violet with a blank expression on her face. Her eyes were red and her face was wrinkled from fatigue.

I heard the sobbing of people from the curtains behind Mona. Emily's parents had returned to check up on their daughter. Emily didn't have much time left, and death often appeared sooner than the doctors could predict. I overheard them talking about money. They hadn't succeeded in raising money for the treatment. They tried applying for a bank loan, but the bank rejected, just as they did with us, since so many families applied for loans now. More and more children became sick. The banks didn't dare to take that risk.

Emily's father made a call and asked if there were any news in selling their house. As he hung up, he started crying out loud, with his wife joining in. I was about to cheer for the good news, but was put down by his next sentence.

"It's not sold."

The desperation in the room was immense. I closed my eyes for a moment, imagining that Violet would open her blue eyes and smile.

"Good morning, Dad," she would say.

"Good morning, little crab," I would reply.

She would sit up in the bed, and I would stroke the blue lines in her hair while listening to her stories from school, and how she would put the mocking guy in place. We would sing our add-on song and add word number 43.

...in a tree - on a branch - with a feather - perfect weather - and a bird - in a nest - with four chicks - eating ticks - having fun...with a Christmas bun..."

Naturally, I wasn't able to add any words. Not without Violet.

The sobbing from the neighbor bed pulled me back to reality. I inspected the necklace in my hand and ran a finger over the violet string before moving my gaze to Mona. Somehow we communicated through our eyes, and she nodded to my request. Emily's parents needed money for the treatment. We had that money, and we had no use for it now.

Mona was the one to deliver the news. That was the only time I ever saw pure, desperate happiness. Emily's parents didn't know how to thank us, and informed that they would pay everything back when they could. I smiled. Mona smiled. This was the moment I realized what I had to do. No other parent should feel the agony of losing a child to that horrible disease! I had to obtain more money. These children needed medicine.

Chapter 12

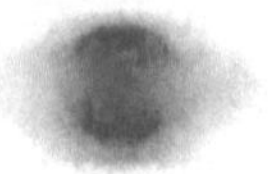

It was right there - the mechanism that would unlock the orb. Freeing the orb would be the act allowing me to escape this entrapment. I still wasn't sure how I would benefit from the orb when we got out, but I didn't doubt its powers. It was capable of doing unimaginable things, and it promised to help fix my problems. I just had to put the orb in the glowing mechanism right in front of me, which appeared to be a simple bowl of luminescent, oily water. The bowl was built into a marble monument shaped as a down-pointing cone, balancing on top of an up-pointing one. Around it was wrapped a thick metal chain, holding it together. At the bottom of the bowl, I spotted a hole only large enough for the orb to fit in.

As I came closer, I felt the mechanism blow bursts of air, as if it was alive and breathing. Everything felt strange as I glanced around the room. There were even more treasures and artifacts here than in the previous places; Enough to save hundreds, if not thousands, of children for years. I considered making a pouch of my clothes to fill with gems, as gold would be too heavy to carry out.

"Do not care about treasures," the orb whispered.

This time I laughed and asked why not. Those treasures were obviously why I was here.

"I am worth far more than gold and gemstones. When I am unlocked, no parent or child will ever worry about diseases. And for your concern, friend, time will never be a problem again."

I was thrilled. I would be the one person who saved thousands of families. When the orb was free, diseases like that would be eliminated. And from what I could understand, the orb could give me more time with my daughter - or at least prevent time from taking her away from me.

"It's time," I was informed.

With the orb between my fingers, I moved my hand to the bowl and dropped it into the strange liquid. The orb shifted to its purple color with golden particles, though this time the light was flickering. As it reached the hole in the bottom, it was sucked down and disappeared. The water blended with a purple substance flowing from the hole, illuminating the whole room with the gloomy color. As the substance took over the water, the golden particles floated up, creating a night-like scenario. The bursts of air from the mechanism were heavy as the ground began to tremble.

"Destroy it! Now!"

The whispering of the orb echoed all over the place. This was it. I only had to break the mechanism, and the orb was free. I unwrapped the chain from the monument and attached it to the handle of a golden jug, which I filled with a handful of golden coins. Hopefully, with the help of the rotating motion from the chain, the jug would be heavy enough to demolish the mechanism in a single blow. I started swinging the chain, and as it reached high speed, I let it jug crash into the balancing marble cone.

All I saw was a glimpse of purple light before I was put to the ground by the imploding force. I did it. The mechanism was destroyed.

dream

I could barely open my eyes when the phone alarm rang on the table in front of me. My body was feeling the effect of working two jobs - being a security guard here in the museum at daytime and a night guard at some important IT company. This was my second week with two jobs, and I was already exhausted. But the night shifts were well paid, and I could save lives with that money. Mona wasn't pleased seeing me destroying myself like that. She thought it was an unhealthy way to deal with sorrow, but she accepted that I wanted to do this. Whenever I was off work, I was either sleeping or weeping with some type of alcohol in my hand. When working, I felt like I had a purpose, now that Violet wasn't here anymore. I wanted to spend my time preventing the disease from hurting people. I was constantly considering how to raise more money to buy medicine for the children who needed it - just until a cure was discovered. For now, working two jobs was the best solution I could think of.

On the way out of the security office, I noticed that the geeks were back in their room. I hadn't seen them for a while. The door was not open wide, as it usually was, so I couldn't watch them this time - but their conversation was loud and clear. The female geek talked about the pollution that was spreading all over town, created by *The Power*. The same subject as I had heard them discuss before, though this time one of the males added that it was the reason why children were getting sick. The third male said what

I was thinking myself:

"We don't have any proof."

These jerks were too much into inventing theories and conspiracies. I knew the type very well from the internet. The type of people who believe that aliens walk amongst us, or that we are simulations created by another intelligence. If they were correct, why wouldn't their information be a common perception?

I was about to continue my security-check routine as something in their conversation caught me by surprise; The female mentioned the medicine for the treatment of the sick children. She claimed that people were blindly buying the medication like it was some magical invention, produced by heroes. People didn't see the reality of what was going on. People didn't question anything. They just kept feeding the cause of the problem. *The Power* was never going to create a cure for this disease.

My anger couldn't take any more of her bullshit. I kicked the door open and yelled at the three startled idiots. I informed them that my daughter died and could have been saved by that *'magical invention'*; I informed them that this *'magical invention'* saved my daughter's friend, who now lives normally because of that; I informed them that this *'magical invention'* fucking saves lives. How dared they?!

"You don't know anything!" I exclaimed before leaving their room.

They didn't have time to respond, as I ran to the toilet and splashed water onto my face. My heart was racing. When I looked up into the mirror, I couldn't recognize myself, seeing a broken man with liquid dripping down every curve and wrinkle on his face. Tears mixed with the water.

"They don't know anything…"

Chapter 13

The shadow was hovering in front of me, large as a full-grown bear. Its shape changed every second, making it impossible for me to see if the freed orb had an actual form. I didn't know what to say, so I just kept staring at the floating shadow while sitting still on the ground. The luminescent liquid from the bowl of the broken mechanism was spread out on the floor, illuminating just enough for me to see the shadow - nothing else. I wasn't scared, yet I wasn't comfortable either. I freed the orb from its prison, just as planned, and now it was going to help me escape and make my life glorious. Why wasn't I thrilled that I for once succeeded in doing something? Why did I feel this empty inside?

The purple liquid on the ground slowly found its way to me. I placed my hand in it and let the strange material run down my wrist, moving it to my face, inspecting the missing fingers. What a small sacrifice for saving so many lives. For some reason, I became curious about how the liquid would taste if I placed a drop on my tongue. It was a piece of knowledge for which I would typically never search. But I was changed. The world was different now. I wanted to learn about things that most people would never think of; They would simply assume that this liquid would taste horrible and poisonous - but they would never know if it truly did.

The shadow moved closer to me, making me remove my hand from my face. Even though it didn't have eyes, I felt it staring directly into my soul. This time I was frightened. Something felt wrong. I realized that I had no control over the orb now. I couldn't just put it in my pocket again. It was free to do whatever it wanted.

"You and I are the same, Christian," it whispered. "We share the same sorrows. We have the same enemy."

I was about to ask, but the shadow saw the question coming.

"Time, Christian. Time is our enemy. It took your daughter. It took your parents. One day it will take you too. Time kills. It will kill even more children. It needs to be stopped."

It took a moment for me to accept that the shadow was right. Time *did* take my daughter from me. It was killing living beings and destroying things that were once built, used and loved. Time *was* the enemy!

"You told me that you are the opposite of time," I said. "What does that mean?"

"You are correct."

I didn't expect a genuine answer to this question, so I decided to let it be.

"If I am correct," I continued. "Is that why time is your enemy?"

The shadow moved right in front of my face. For a split-second, I saw the hint of a tearing eye in one of the shifting shapes. Perhaps I even heard the low sound of a cry.

"I have been kept imprisoned for eternities. That was a result of time. Time has ruled for just as long as I have been hidden away. Now it is my turn to rule. I will prevail!"

I stood up from the ground, while the shadow became just as tall as I. For a moment, it felt like staring into a demonic mirror, and I was terrified.

"Can you bring my daughter back?" I asked.

The shadow started laughing. The laughter was deep enough to make the ground tremble. I felt the vibrations in my chest, making it hard for me to breathe. When the shadow finally spoke, the voice was just as deep and loud.

"You humans are so naive. Stupid as beasts, and easily manipulated."

I couldn't believe it.

"You lied all this time?!" I exclaimed.

"What did I have to lose? I got what I wanted; My freedom; My chance to take back the power. You thought you were important, but you were never more than a puppet. But I tell you this, Christian; You are the reason for my success."

The rage took control of me. I grabbed the chain and swung the golden jug into the shadow, but it went right through. The echoes from the shadow's laughter pierced my ears as I attempted to assemble the mechanism again. It didn't work. I couldn't bear the feeling of betrayal. *I wouldn't accept it!*

"Fight me, you coward!" I roared and let my purple fist fly towards the shadow.

The laughter died and turned into a horrifying screech as I hit the shadow. Instantly, I was pushed backward and landed hard on the ground. The shadow hovered over the purple liquid until it began vaporizing. It took only a few seconds before the liquid was gone and the cave was left completely dark. Everything became quiet. The last thing I heard was a whisper in my ear:

"Goodbye, Christian."

dream

As with the previous days, I awoke on the couch, thirty minutes before my nightshift started at the IT company. The television was still running and showed the credits of some dull movie which the TV channel decided to show. I sipped from the cup of cold coffee on the table. Five cups of coffee definitely wouldn't be enough to get through the shift tonight; I had to increase the dosage a cup or two. I guess my body was telling me to get a night of proper sleep, but that could wait till the weekend.

"Evening, love," Mona greeted as she arrived home. "Ready for work?"

I arose from the couch and hugged her tight. For some reason, I was happy to see her that night. I kissed her soft lips and told her that I loved her. I embraced her chin while gently biting her lower lip, smelling the sweet perfume she always wore. She removed herself from me with a curious smile on her face.

"What's with you today? Something happened?" she asked.

"I missed you."

She chuckled and blushed, just like when I bought her roses when we were young and newly in love. Apparently, she had been urging for me to say simple things like that, as she went in for another hug. I couldn't remember when was the last time I felt this way about Mona. I loved her, that was certain. However, the hole in my heart wasn't filled - it could never be. When Mona kissed me farewell and went for the shower, and I sat down on the couch to drink the remaining cold coffee, I feared that I would never feel genuine happiness again.

The TV showed an advertisement I hadn't seen before. First at the end, I realized what it tried to sell: medication. The same treatment as Violet and all the other children needed. How did they manage to get such an ad broadcasted on the television? Were they *that* desperate to sell their expensive medicine? Did they expect some other brand to compete against them?

The alarm rang on my phone; I had to get going. Looking out the window, I noticed the thick layer of fog hovering on the street.

...fog....

I tried recalling the last time I saw a similar view from my window, but couldn't think of any. It didn't seem right. After a bit of consideration, I picked up the phone and called someone I never called before.

"Hi Pete, it's Christian. I'm sorry about my attack on you guys today. I need to speak with you."

A Love Story

Christian observed the new girl as she entered the room and found her name on the table next to him. At the end of fifth grade, it was announced that a new girl arrived in town and would join the class after the summer holiday. They never informed that she would be this pretty, Christian thought. He had never been in love before. He never even kissed a girl - or a boy for that matter. The new girl should turn out to be the one changing his life.

"I'm Mona," she said when she discovered that her class-neighbor was staring at her.

Christian was a shy, young man and looked away as soon as he realized his mesmerized condition. The new girl, Mona, giggled. From the corner of his eye, Christian noticed the blushing of her cheeks. She already knew that he liked her, but he didn't know about her interest in him. She saw, from the nametag on his table, that his name was Thomas. It took him a week before he dared to tell her, that his name was actually Christian, and that he swapped tables with Thomas because Thomas wanted to sit next to Eric. Christian didn't have many friends in school, and especially not Eric, so he had no reason not to change seats.

Christian didn't speak much with Mona for the next couple of months, even though they were neighbors in class. She often tried to get his attention, but he always became nervous and retreated. It annoyed him. Why couldn't he just talk to this girl? He felt a rush in his stomach every time he looked at her; When he heard her speak with that exotic, British accent; When he dreamt of her cool, colorful clothes. What he didn't know was that their heart rates synchronized whenever they were in the same room.

It was first at the annual Christmas party, at school, that they became official friends. Christian was sitting alone on a couch, sipping his third soda, watching the girls on the dancefloor. He didn't see Mona dancing and worried that she was being held hostage by Eric's flirting. The thought was unbearable. First of all, because Eric was a mocking idiot, but also, as Christian now understood, because jealousy is nothing but torture. He wished that his only classmate was here, but he never went to gatherings like these. Christian was just about to leave the couch when Mona bumped down next to him. She grinned, being loaded with sugar and uncontrolled feelings. This time she would make sure that he couldn't escape. Christian's palms were moisty and his voice trembled as he replied to her questions. The soda bottle in his lab was an excellent focal point when speaking, as she looked way too beautiful that night. When she took his hand, he panicked and pulled it back, but she was quick and took a firm hold of it. Mona decided that it was time. She leaned in and kissed him on his mouth. An act that would turn out to be the beginning of a love story.

Christian and Mona dated for many years. Everything seemed more than perfect for both of them. They knew that their love was ordinary, but they felt it unique. Mona and Christian were to be together forever - or so they thought.

The two were growing and preparing to become adults. Mona got a once-in-a-lifetime opportunity to enter a Fine Arts school back in England, and Christian wanted to travel and gain experience to study archeology, as his grades weren't good enough.

Mona decided for them that they would have to break up.

"Long distance relationships are painful," she said. "It will destroy us."

Christian was broken and tried to change her mind. He would forget about archaeology and come with her to England. She was the most important thing in the world. What he didn't know was that he was the most important thing for her too, and she couldn't bear to destroy his dreams of archeology. She couldn't bear missing him for so long either. Breaking up was the only solution.

Mona studied for three years, wherein she dated a dozen different guys. She loved her studies. She loved being back in England. The only thing she didn't enjoy was how she felt when being with other men, why she dated so many. She longed for that sparkling feeling; The feeling of being in love.

Christian backpacked Europe for six months before returning to Canada. The traveling had given him a positive view of the world, but not enough experience or knowledge to get into the studies he wanted. The disappointed young man decided to buy a ton of archeology books, which he would read until he was allowed into education. After two and a half years, the books had rarely been opened, as the jobs he worked were tiring. When getting off work, all he managed to do was to lie on his bed and think of Mona. Some evenings he cried. Sometimes he found a picture of her and smiled. On one particular evening, he made up his mind.

The day Mona graduated from Art School was a Tuesday. The color of her dress that day was violet, which became the inspiration later on. She was greeted by her family, who had traveled from Canada to celebrate her, when she exited the enormous double doors of the school. The sun was shining and everything felt great. They drove to Mona's apartment, where they ate and drank all evening. Mona dropped the news that she decided to stay in England for some time. The family wasn't thrilled, but they accepted it. She was a free woman, after all. When her parents left for their hotel in the night, they kissed her goodbye and agreed to meet with her the next day.

The sudden silence baffled Mona. She wasn't sure why, but she didn't feel genuinely happy. When the door phone rang and she heard the familiar voice greet her, she almost couldn't believe it. Christian went up the stairs with flowers in his hand, which he handed to her. At first, she blushed. Then she laughed. Not because she thought it funny, but because she needed this laughter. Christian was confused but laughed with her. He felt it a bit awkward. On his way there, he pictured a romantic love-scene, like those from movies where two people, who are meant to be together, meet after several years; They'd jump into each other's arms and perform the most intense kisses of their lives. This reunion wasn't like that at all. However, at the end of that night, Christian found it to be the best of his life.

Well, that was just until a few years later, when violet was born. Mona had moved back to Canada with Christian, and her parents loved him for it. At that moment, Christian couldn't care less about archeology. He had the two loves of his life's right there in front of him. For what more could he wish?

Chapter 14

Something slapped me hard on the face. Panicking, I jumped right into the arms of a muscular, furry creature, which took a firm hold of me. The fire of a torch behind me allowed me to see the face of the creature. It reminded me of a grizzly bear, though thinner and with jet-black eyes. Two large fangs were showing from its mouth. The tight grip made it impossible for me to fight. I was tired and hungry - and I found that death might not be that bad after all. When the pain of having those fangs penetrating my flesh was over, I would be at peace. My time would be over. That annoying time!

To my surprise, the creature put me down on the ground, releasing me. The burning torch moved in front, together with its owner. Was I hallucinating? Was it really a human?

"My name is Lumit," the young woman said, with a voice reminding me of butter.

She had black, long hair hanging loose from her head, and a mild, innocent face. The beige robe with golden ornaments revealed that she was some kind of monk, yet I didn't know much about such types of people. What touched me was her eyes; I saw Violet in her blue eyes. She had Violet's eyes! That couldn't be - this woman was not caucasian. I must be losing my mind. Nevertheless, I *did* ask her if she was my daughter, but she rejected the idea.

"What is your name?" she asked.

"My name is Christian Hawkin," I informed.

She inspected me for a while. I noticed the dagger in her hand and assumed that she was considering whether to kill me or not. If the blade wouldn't kill me, the bear behind her would.

"Why did you unleash the content of the orb?" she asked.

I told her everything. I told her how I awoke in here with no memory, and how I found the orb who played me since the minute it spoke to me. I told her about the fights with the creatures and the loss of my fingers. When I came to the part of fighting the shadow, she interrupted;

"I heard enough."

She lit another torch and handed it to me. The light from the two flaming sticks illuminated the entire space, revealing a dozen strange creatures standing in a circle around us. They all reminded me of familiar animals, yet very different. One creature reminded me of a lone wolf with the fur of bronze-colored needles. Another creature appeared like an enormous worm-like snake. A third had the body of a gigantic raccoon, but with grey and black feathers instead of fur. They all had one thing in common: the jet-black eyes. The creatures weren't as frightening when idling and observing like that. Why didn't they attack?

"I was summoned by the beings you see around us," the monk, Lumit, informed. "They tried to stop you from following your orders, but the power of the orb was too strong."

"That's why my life was spared when the orb was taken?"

"The beings mean you no harm. They are here to prevent the unnatural element of the orb from escaping, but failed."

A feeling of guilt rushed through my body. What had I done?

"We need to prevent it from escaping," Lumit commanded. "The exit must be sealed before it's found."

"What will happen if we don't?"

She looked me deep in the eyes.

"It will be the end of time. The shadow of the orb seeks to destroy everything natural on it's hunt to obtain more power."

"The shadow said it was the opposite of time? Is that natural?"

"No. However, it's a natural habit to fight for power, but when much power is gained, and more is desired, all natural fail while all unnatural prevail. The unnatural must be kept hidden, as its lies will destroy and kill."

I didn't understand the words, but I understood their meaning. Everything suddenly made sense. How could I have been so blind? I should never have trusted in false promises and lies from the orb and its powers. I should have used my head and questioned if its motives were genuine - if it truly wanted to help me, and not take advantage of me.

Lumit performed some kind of sign language to the creatures, and they left in different directions, one by one. I figured they were to hunt down the shadow before it found its way to the exit. Only the bear was left when she turned to me.

"The three of us will head directly for the exit to seal it," she informed. "Hopefully it's not too late."

She had a necklace around her neck, which she waved in the air before holding it still, inspecting. Attached was a small glass sphere with grains of metallic sand inside. She rotated the necklace a couple of times before stepping forward, determined where to go. The bear followed behind as she walked at a fast pace into a narrow passage. I started following the bear, keeping a bit of distance. Right before entering the passage, I saw the arrow scratched into the ground - pointing in the direction we were headed. The creature, who created the arrow, simply wanted me to leave when it took the orb. The guilt grew inside of me. The shadow had to be stopped!

dream

I was staring blankly into the screensaver of a bubble floating around the laptop screen. How long had I been sitting like this? Pete arrived at my side and put a hand on my shoulder.

"You look like you need this," he said while filling up my coffee cup.

I thanked him again. I still felt horrible for raging out at these guys at work earlier, but when I arrived here at Pete's apartment, they accepted my apology right away. They invited me to explain everything I had been through, and they assured me that they would have acted the same way if being in my situation. I couldn't believe that I never talked to these guys before. I always just saw them as geeks - maybe because of jealousy, who knows? Pete was the only one I had conversed with a few times before, and when I think back on it, I found him quite friendly back then. His green eyes were intense, along with the fiery, long hair. Mia and Max turned out to be just as great. First now, I learned that their nerdy accents and blond appearances were German, and apparently, they were married to each other; They didn't hold back their opinions when talking to each other, at least.

After I emptied my heart on the poor guys, they informed me of all their theories and hypotheses. They showed me their newly-found proof that the medicine company was the cause of the disease, though it wasn't strong enough evidence to bust the industry. The smog filling up the city didn't awake people, as the industry had a foot in the butt of the newspapers, radio- and TV-news. Officially, the smog was a naturally developed fog caused by a humid climate that year. The weather forecasts never showed that the humidity was higher than usual, but no one - including myself - ever questioned the missing connection to the news. The common assumption was that the media was reliable and announced genuine news which people could trust and make their own perception. The information from these guys was an eye-opener, and I was convinced they were correct. I shouldn't collect money to buy medicine and keep the business going - I should stop the cause of the disease for good.

The clock in the corner of the computer screen revealed that we had been brainstorming and researching ideas for six hours. It was time for another discussion. Pete was the first to speak;

"Well, we all know that the four of us solely can't defeat an enormous industry such as The Power."

"I suggest we demolish the factory!" Max interrupted.

I found that Max was a bit more radical than Mia, who was way more radical than Pete, who was like me. Pete was often the one who put down their extreme suggestions;

"They will just build it up again."

"What if we assassinate the idio…" Mia proposed, but was cut off by Pete.

"Not a solution, Mia."

"But they are killing children!"

Exactly! I knew her desperation and was about to vote good for the proposal when Pete continued.

"Killing is not an option. The population believes that these people in the industry are heroes, and they will fight against us if it comes down to murder."

"We have to convince the population that they are being lied to," I added, as I now understood where he was going. "We have to make them believe in the truth."

"But they don't listen to a minority like us!" Mia exclaimed. "They are blind and have always been!"

She was right. Her words left us all wondering. Obviously, we shouldn't start murdering people or vandalizing buildings. The best option was to let us, the minority, become the majority by convincing people of the truth. But how would that be possible?

"What do The Power have that we don't?" Pete asked.

"Money?" I proposed.

"That's right! And how does The Power control the opinions of the population?"

"Media? News?"

"And what does it take to control the media and the news?"

"Money!"

I stood up from my chair. Pete's expression told me that he knew I was with him. Money was what made The Power so powerful.

"We fight power with power!" I pronounced.

"But how?" Mia asked.

That was when the idea popped into my head. I knew exactly where that power could be achieved. It would be illegal and somewhat dangerous, but what had I to lose? I didn't doubt if Max and Mia were in on the idea - they were radical enough - but would Pete be interested?

"I have to show you something," I said and turned to my laptop.

The group gathered around me as I typed in "India."

Chapter 15

We had been running for hours. Occasionally, we ran into large marble doors, which Lumit opened, only by throwing some sort of silverish dust on them and moving her hand. When I asked, all I got for a reply was "*Magnetism*" - and then more running. As if such an answer didn't raise more questions in my head, but I didn't dare to ask for further explanation.

We reached an enormous boulder blocking the way; The shadow was ahead of us, trying to slow us down. The bear attempted to move the huge rock, but it was too heavy. After a few attempts, Lumit signed for the bear to move, and she started working on the boulder herself. This was the ideal time for me to have my curiosity satisfied.

"Lumit," I started. "What exactly was in that orb? How did it end up there?"

She continued inspecting the boulder while answering.

"It took only time to overcome and entrap the powerful shadow that once ruled the universe," she replied. "It has been that way for nearly fourteen billion years."

From her pocket, she picked up two golden cubes, attaching one to the boulder and placing the other one on the ground in front.

"It took only time?" I mumbled. "Time killed my daughter!"

The shadow was correct with this one. I just needed a bit more time and my daughter would still be alive. Time didn't allow us to raise the money for medicine. Time took my daughter from me. It took my dad. It took my childhood dog. In time we will all die. Time kills. Time *is* the enemy!

"Time kept your daughter alive," Lumit said. "Time creates life, moments, motions. Without time, there is no life. Naturally, like everything else in the universe, time isn't perfect, why you can't blame it for it's faults."

"I don't understand…"

She turned around and looked at me.

"Time didn't kill your daughter, Christian; The opposite did. You *had* time with her - now you have *none*. Which do you prefer?"

I stayed quiet.

"You see, time is good if you appreciate it. Don't stress about it. Don't measure it without reason. Don't think about it when you don't have to. Just enjoy it while you have it."

She turned around and fiddled with her golden cubes again.

Only now, I realized how she was right; I urged for *more time* with Violet. I loved the time I had with her. I wished she had more time in the world. That led me to a naive idea;

"Can you control time?" I asked.

"No mortal can control time alone. Your decisions direct your own portion of time, and to some degree it can affect the time of others. Time listens to you and adapts, like a friend."

While I reflected on the information, Lumit covered the boulder in some of her metallic dust and connected the ground cube with a fine line of the glittering powder. She sat on her knees and touched the cube. With help from the bear, the boulder now moved sideways, in a slow, fluent motion, until there was a gap large enough for us all to fit through.

"Now, we don't have much time left," she announced. "We need to take full use of it. Let's go!"

dream

Turbulence caused me to pull off my eye-mask. Mia, Max and Pete were still sleeping, despite all other passengers seeming to have awakened from the bouncing of the airplane. I grabbed my phone and checked the time; Only two hours left until arriving in Bangalore, Southern India. I noticed the small icon at the top of the screen, showing that I had an unread message. It must have been received before we took off. The message was from Mona. "Be careful, Christian," was all it said.

Before I managed to become emotional, another round of turbulence came to my rescue. The trembling was strong enough to pull my phone out of my hand, down the floor, where it disappeared under the seat in front. Max, who was sitting next to me, let out a loud snore as if he was annoyed by the aircraft trying to mess with his sleep. How these guys could keep sleeping was unknown to me - though I had a theory that the sleeping pills had a stronger effect on them.

The atmosphere in the cabin was strange. People looked frightened, and the tense mood spread like a plague and devoured all hopes of a joyful flight. As I bent down to search for my phone, my head crashed right into the seat in front. To be fair, it didn't quite hurt, as the thing was made of cheap plastic, but it didn't improve my mood either. As I thought things couldn't get worse, the annoying, wrinkled woman in that seat turned around and glanced over the seat's top before she muttered if I *could please stop that?* Faster than I succeeded in reacting, her head disappeared as she sat down again, bumping her back aggressively into the seat. At first, I brushed off her braindead comment and giggled to myself. Then her reaction repeated in my head, while the tense mood returned. In the end, I was filled with frustration and anger. I wanted to yell at the idiot - tell her to ease off - or to jump out the plane instead of being such a depressing, old witch. I thought of so many comebacks that would shut the crone's toothless mouth. Why didn't I just say something? It was too late now, but the rage was still building up inside me. I decided to try and let it go, managing to sweep up my phone from under her seat and snake my way back up without touching anything. The screen was cracked from the corner, all the way down the middle. I shook my head in denial.

Of course, the phone didn't work properly now, so whenever my finger touched the screen, the touch-sensor was slightly off and misclicked. All I wanted was to find a picture of Violet, yet I wasn't sure if I wished to remind myself why we were doing this, or if I hoped for a happy memory to cheer me up. When I finally got the image folder open, more forceful turbulence arrived. The seatbelt sign blinked off and on, while the bell chimed, reminding people to stay attached to their seats. The noisy engines next to the wings intensified, and in the chaos I felt the flight attempting to ascent. This time Max awoke and grabbed his armrests, while his head was bobbing like crazy. His eyes glowed from contagious fear.

Terrified, I worked to open one of the images of Violet, but the trembling and faulty touchscreen resulted in the image being deleted. *NO!*

"What's happening?" Max stuttered.

I didn't have time to answer. If the plane was going down, I wanted to smile by the happy face of Violet, just one last time.

The plane was dropping. Babies were crying. Adults shrieked. Max cramped up and held his breath. In desperation, I fiddled with the phone until an image finally popped up. It was of Violet and me in the woods. For a moment, the shaking and panic disappeared, and I was back in the green forest. The birds were singing. The fresh air filled my nostrils with the scent of grass and wildflowers. Violet sang our song … *with a Christmas bun!* … while the sun illuminated her beautiful, wavy hair with its vibrant blue lines. She grinned at me. I laughed. I felt so happy - so complete. How did I ever deserve to be granted such a treasure? The love of my life.

"Christian?" Max murmured, pulling me back to reality.

The aircraft was steady again and the panic was over. It turned out to be nothing but heavy turbulence. I removed my eyes from the screen and met Max's. Realizing that tears were rushing down my chin, I opened my mouth to speak, but no words escaped. I couldn't say a thing. What was I supposed to say? Max's expression became of sorrow as he noticed the image on my phone.

"We are doing a great thing," he said. "We *will* succeed!"

His words gave me strength. He was right. The Power was to be suppressed and eliminated! When we would succeed in obtaining the resources to fight, people would finally open their eyes and turn against them. All we had to do was to enter the locked vault and collect the treasures. I remembered the first time I heard about the Padmanabhaswamy temple and the vaults it contained. The vaults were opened and had billions of dollars in coins, gemstones and other ancient treasures. Only *one* vault - Vault B - remained sealed. The entrance contained three doors, whereas the last one, an enormous iron door, indicated *danger*. Wise monks feared that a curse would spread if forced open, and numerous rumors told that people who tried to enter were brutally killed. Even the government decided to protect the vault from intrusion, despite the fact that wealth beyond imagination might be found. It was a decision which an atheist like me, with interest in such artifacts, never fully understood. Nevertheless, with only a tiny portion of this wealth, we would be able to create a strong resistance to make the truth about The Power - the medicine industry - common knowledge. The remaining sick children would receive free medicine while an antidote development was ongoing. When the medical industry was suppressed, who would know what other devastating industries were the next targets. The world would be clean and honest - without greed and the urge for power. No more lies. No more egoism. No more killing and destroying to gain wealth.

I closed my eyes and exhaled with pleasure. We *would* succeed!

Chapter 16

My legs couldn't follow. I lost sight of Lumit and the bear, so I decided to pause in the strange, white room in an attempt to catch my breath. After a minute of gasping, with my hands on my thighs, I was ready to start running again, but as I moved the torch back up to illuminate the doorway, I saw that there were now *three* doorways. As I approached, I realized that the white walls were made of bones; Some big, some small, some the size of human body parts. When studying them up close, I figured that they were held in place by some kind of solid web.

Looking back from where I entered, I saw three similar doorways. The two remaining walls also contained three doorways each. As I turned around to the doorway I was heading for, I lost all sense of direction. I had no clue which was the correct one, and from which I came. The sound of my voice seemed faint when I called out for Lumit. The walls absorbed almost all sound, and the lack of ambiance resulted in a weird pressure around my head. There was no way that Lumit could hear me.

I tried recalling how many rotations I had made in the room to backtrack my movement, but I simply couldn't remember. If only I knew from where I entered. The door openings all looked the same and were basically just holes in the bony walls, yet each doorway had a human skull above. In the middle of the room was a marble tomb with screaming skulls engraved, blocking their ears with skeletal fingers. I wouldn't be surprised if the tomb contained something horrible, so I took a moment to listen for sounds, but heard nothing.

When I least expected it, the lack of sound became an explosion of simultaneous screaming and aggressive yelling from hundreds of voices owned by all ages and genders, from high-pitched children, to deep-voiced men, to older women. They repeated the same thing over and over;

"Wake up! Wake up! Wake up! ..."

I couldn't stand it and tried to protect my ears, but the voices went right through my hands. Insanity was close.

"Wake up! Wake up! ..."

I shouted and begged the voices to stop, but they kept yelling!

"Wake up! ..."

I didn't care which door I took, as long as I escaped this madness. With my lungs being emptied from roaring, I ran for the closest doorway. The second I stepped out of the room, the voices stopped, but I kept sprinting the fastest I could. I must have run faster than the speed of light, as the torch didn't illuminate the ground in front of me, but I wasn't prepared to stop any time soon. I hinted a warm glow in the distance, getting more intense as I fought my way towards it, knowing that it was the light from Lumit's torch. However, as soon as I reached, I was attacked by the aggressive voices again.

"Wake up! ..."

I found myself in another bony room, lit by torches attached to skeletal hands reaching out of the walls. The room had four doors on each wall, sealed with the same strange web holding the walls in place. A similar tomb was in the middle, with dead trees carved into it. I wanted to return the way I came, but again I lost sense of direction. The attempt to block out the voices with my hands didn't succeed, and insanity built up even faster than before, so I brought my torch to the closest web blockade and saw it melt away with a vibrant, green glow. An intense wind built up in the room and before I knew it, I was sucked right through the doorway and through a narrow, silent passage. I tried grabbing for the walls, but the force of the wind was too strong. I had to give in and let it lead me to wherever it wanted.

I heard the voices return and was pushed into the middle of yet another room built of skeleton parts. The voices were louder than ever, led by the shrill voice of an elderly, mental woman, and my head was about to explode. This room had five doorways on each wall, and the torches illuminating it was held by skeletal arms growing from the ground, encircling the tomb; This one had an eye carved into each side. Without further consideration, I sprinted towards one of the doorways but slammed my head right into some invisible field. The voices shouted even louder.

"Wake up!! …"

What was I supposed to do? I tried kicking the door open, but only hurt my leg with a cracking pain. I tried spitting in an attempt to dissolve the field with liquid, but that didn't do it either. Roaring from ear-deafening agony, I searched for hidden buttons or levers, but found nothing.

"What am I supposed to do?!" I cried while falling to a sitting position.

I felt a tooth break from the clenching of my teeth, sending a sharp pain from my jaw to my ear. The taste of salt and bitter rot took over my mouth as I checked the tooth with my dirty finger. I managed to pull a piece out, feeling the nerves' signals pulsing of danger. Like a mad man, I tossed it on the ground. My tongue removed the remaining tooth, while my eyes were forced shut, my mouth spitting the bloody thing out the air. It took a moment before the pain eased enough for me to open my eyes again. The line of blood from my spitting position, to where the tooth had fallen, was long and thick. I couldn't even see where it had landed.

Suddenly I jumped up from the ground; The tooth had landed on the other side of a doorway! I realized that all the doorways had bones crossed like an X above them - all but one. I was so focused on getting through this single door that I forgot about the others. This other doorway didn't contain an invisible blockage, and I walked right past it without a problem. The voices stopped immediately as I found myself standing in front of a huge stairway. The light from my torch didn't reach the top, so I couldn't know how long it was, and I didn't feel like hurrying, fearing that it just led to another room of screaming voices. But I wasn't allowed to have a break, as the tomb cracked open in the skeletal room, and the ground filled with long-legged spiders. Jumping up on the first step, I continued upwards. My speed was fast, and I tripped several times on the way, but kept a steady pace; Until the stairs ended while I tripped over a soft object and fell for who knows how long.

It took a moment before I pulled myself up from the ground and removed dirt from my new bruises. The small object, which caused my fall, was lying naked in front of me. The instance I picked it up, I remembered; I knew what this brown pouch was, and what it contained. Pete gave it to me. Suddenly, I recalled being in this place before. I looked to my side and saw the edge of an enormous drop leading to complete darkness. Moving there, I stretched my arm out, with the torch in my hand, and looked down… Yes, there they were - Pete, Mia and Max - the three dead people I found when I awoke in this place.

I remembered everything. I had discovered the orb, and the

guys wanted me to get rid of it. They knew about its lies, but I was blind. The orb gave me false hopes of bringing my daughter back, and I believed, like a child believing in the tooth fairy. This was *my* fault. I didn't listen to them. I ended up fighting them, resulting in every single one of us falling. The orb had played me the entire time. Now one of the its speeches echoed in my head:

"Does it change what you're about to do, if you know what happened in this place? Does it change your emotions if you remember who you were before this place? Does it change your current longings if you know what happened before you ended up here?"

Only then, I realized how important the past actually was. Naturally, I couldn't change the past, but learning from it was the key. The orb convinced me that the moment was most important, and to some degree it was right; When not knowing the past, the past won't control your feelings and wishes. The moment *was* important, but that moment was now my agony; Knowing that I had a part in killing my friends - in supporting the killing of children - in the death of Violet. How could I live with these memories in the future? The past now controlled my emotions completely. The memories tightened my heart - though, somewhere inside of me, I was unsure if the memories were truly from the past, how silly that must sound.

dream

The smoke from my cigarette dissolved in the warm breeze as I blew tiny clouds from my lips. The silence was strange, after being trapped in a bouncy plane, and later in a bus full of screaming babies and their conversing parents. Now we finally had arrived in the village.

"I didn't know you smoked," Pete said, joining me outside the hotel entrance.

"My first cigarette ever," I admitted. "People smoke to relax, and I thought I would give it a try."

"Is it working for you then?" Pete chuckled.

I tossed the remaining cigarette.

"Not really my thing."

We stood in silence for a while, just enjoying the peace. Mia and Max were sleeping in their hotel room, but I was too anxious to lie in a bed. My body was full of stress and doubt, which was the reason for the desperate smoking attempt.

"Are you sharing?" Pete asked and pointed at the pack of beers at my feet.

I completely forgot about those beers. Picking and opening two, I handed one to Pete.

"Cheers, my friend," I said, in a failed attempt to sound cheerful.

We both sipped, again letting the silence rule for a moment.

"I know it can't compare to your story," Pete began. "But I

once lost a loved one too."

I stayed mute, giving Pete the time to explain.

"My brother," he continued. "He was like me - like us - striving to do good things in the world; Trying to bust industries and enlighten the population."

He sipped his beer like he was considering if he should continue with the story or not.

"What happened?" I asked, indicating that I was listening.

His voice was trembling now, fighting not to cry.

"The industry he fought had a connection to the government, in a country where government business results in disappearances. One day he just wasn't there anymore. No calls, no information, no police investigations. Nothing."

From the corner of my eye, I spotted a tear running down his chin.

"That's one of the things making the industries strong," he continued. "There are no limits to what their money can do, and what they are willing to do, to avoid getting caught."

"And people believe in their lies," I added.

Pete removed the tear and looked at me.

"Why did we never talk before?"

The sentence put a smile on my face. I pulled him in for a hug; A hug that we both needed at this moment; A hug that went on for a while. After releasing each other, we cheered again, but this time, I actually sounded cheerful. Pete put a hand in his pocket and pulled up a little brown pouch.

"If you ever doubt what we're doing here," he said and put it in my hand. "This will aid you. Never be afraid. What we are doing is good."

I stared at the pouch with a strange feeling of deja vu; The beer must have been stronger than expected. My curiosity wanted to check the content, but I decided to put the pouch in my pocket instead. I sipped again.

"You know," Pete continued. "The world is strange. Sometimes I'm not sure if I'm dreaming or not."

"I know the feeling, my friend," I admitted. "I know the feeling very well."

Chapter 17

Lumit found me rolled up on the ground next to the edge of the deep drop. The bear had to drag me up, like a kid not getting its way. Lumit studied me.

"Christian, wake up. We need you," she claimed, but I didn't listen.

How could she need me? How could anybody in the world need *me*?

"Christian!" Lumit growled. "This is bigger than you! It's not too late, but we need you - *now*!"

She ended the sentence with a slap in my face. Not a strong one, but enough for me to realize the situation. My eyes flicked and eventually met hers.

"What do you need me for?"

She led me through a long, tortuous passage until we ended up at a huge cave opening. I couldn't believe my eyes. In it were hundreds of lightning strikes, continually flashing throughout the whole space. It reminded me of the neverending Catatumbo Lightning in Venezuela, just a lot more intense. This was obviously not ordinary lightning. The strikes were white, but the glow was of various pastel colors. Luminous, pastel clouds floated in the ceiling, from which the lightning was generated.

"We can not cross this area one by one," Lumit informed. "But together, we have a chance."

I assumed that a single strike would kill us, as I felt the energy in the air, even though we weren't even close. A cold wind formed in the chaos.

"How are we going to stop the lightning?" I asked.

"We're not. We are going through it."

I had to check if she was serious, but her face showed no signs of joy. I even glanced at the bear in the hope of it revealing a smile, but it only stared back at me with a tilted head.

"If you look at the ground," Lumit continued. "You will see circular lodestones. They will protect and guide us."

I narrowed my eyes and noticed that the ground contained pieces of clean metal built into the floor. But I had to remove my eyes again, as the lightning flashes were too painful to watch.

"Take off your shoes," she continued.

I didn't dare to question her. As I bent down to untie my shoes, I realized that they didn't have laces. Reflecting on when I lost those laces, I took off the shoes and placed them to the side. Lumit was already barefoot herself.

"Here, bring your hand to this."

She held a golden cube out, on which I placed my hand. It was cold and felt like regular gold - or at least what I assumed a gold cube would feel like.

"You can not let go of this cube," Lumit informed. "If either of us loses touch, we are both dead. Do you understand?"

With fear glowing from my eyes, I nodded.

"Likewise is it required that both of us have at least one foot on a lodestone at any time," she continued with an expression telling me that she was serious. "If we work together, and don't lose connection with either the cube or the lodestones, then the strikes will not harm us."

I moved my gaze to the pastel-colored strikes.

"What happens if only one of us has a foot down?" I asked,

just to be sure.

"Instant death."

I regretted asking.

"And there is no other way? How did you enter yourself?"

"I am allowed," she replied. "These measures are for intruders and captives. How the shadow managed to overcome this is beyond my knowledge. But we don't have much time, Christian. We have to move."

"What about the bear?"

"Alone, he is not directly affected by the lightning," she informed while taking a step closer to the flashing area. "Just don't touch him!"

Standing right in front of the strikes, we both stepped a foot out on a lodestone while keeping our hands on the golden cube. The lightning struck me over and over, and I felt a slight burn in my spine each time the energy ran through my bones, but nothing serious.

Lumit moved her back foot in front, placed it on a lodestone and indicated that I was to do the same. As I moved my back foot in front, I almost lost balance, but managed to regain it. Lumit cleared her throat and nodded at the cube; Only the tips of my fingers were placed on it, so I instantly moved my whole hand and took a firm hold.

"Sorry," I mumbled, sweat starting to form on my forehead.

With the colorful glow from the bright flashes surrounding her, I saw Lumit lift what was now her rear foot, but this time I copied her movement, raising my own rear foot in a steady motion. We both moved our foot in front and placed them on each of our lodestones. Then we repeated the maneuver - again and again, while the strikes made sure to keep us alert. The bear was already on the other side of the lightning area when I begged for a one-minute break to get control of my nerves.

Looking back, I found that we were halfway. This wasn't that difficult. Everything would be okay. In a few minutes, we should be clear of the electric chaos, and then what could be worse?

"Okay, I'm ready," I informed.

Lumit nodded and we continued our stepping sequence, one foot at a time. But something felt wrong. I noticed the color red on the ground every time I lifted my right foot. Step by step, the pain came sneaking. After a minute, it was unbearable. Each step felt as if a nail was being forced into the ball of my foot. Each step brought more blood. I wanted to stop and remove whatever was the cause, but before I could alert Lumit, I slipped in the pool of liquid flowing from my foot. I barely realized that both my hands took off from the fall, before the first lightning stroke, paralyzing every muscle in my body. I heard the golden cube fall to the ground just before I was hit again, burning from my feet, up my spine, through my eyes and into my brain. All my eyes could see were glimpses of Lumit on the ground. The bear was pulling her, both of them being roasted by the smoking lightning, striking them over and over. I felt my own body being dragged. Every time the strikes hit, my body twitched and the air was punched out of my lungs. I couldn't move. I couldn't think. All I felt was wrenching agony.

Everything was still blurry, as I managed to sit up on the ground. I was saved. So was Lumit, apparently. I heard her speak, yet my ears couldn't make out the words. By the blurred shape, it appeared that she was sitting on her knees, bending over something. Narrowing my eyes, I saw the bear on the ground in front of her. It wasn't moving, but I could hear heavy breaths. Lumit put a hand on its head.

"Sleep well, my friend."

Then the breathing stopped and Lumit put her head to the animal. I wanted to apologize, but I couldn't speak. What words could make up for this anyway?

I closed my eyes for just a second. When I reopened them, I saw a hand flying right into my face, slamming hard and loud on my chin. The result was overwhelming, as I was now fully awake, able to see and hear clearly again. Lumit dropped a lit torch on the ground next to me.

"The exit is close," she informed. "Get up! We have to move fast!"

dream

I stood up, put on shoes, went outside and moved down the walking street. I had never been to India before, and it was nothing like I imagined it to be. This wasn't a big city like those you see on videos, with smog, honking and traffic going in all directions. This was surely a busy street, people walking fast with purpose, but without hard traffic and the noise that follows. The temperature was warm, but not burning, as it was quite early. The sky was blue with a few orange clouds, colored by the still-rising sun. The settings couldn't be much better, but I still felt hazy. Maybe some breakfast would do good.

While continuing down the street, I kept an eye open for a clean street food stall, or at least for a good cup of coffee. Most stalls were still opening up, while the open ones weren't of my interest; As always, I was choosy when it came to food.

A young woman with thick long hair waved at me and smiled when I passed her stall. I returned a timid smile and a nod while walking by. Then a grey-bearded man stopped and watched me with a smirk on his face. It was apparent that he wasn't used to seeing strangers like me in this part of town, just staring curiously. As I passed him, I sent him a smile and a nod as well, while the man took off his Indian hat and greeted me before moving on himself.

I then passed a young couple sitting up against a yellow building, holding each other's arms. She was crying as he spoke. A younger man was watching them with sad eyes from the neighbor building. I wished to know what was going on, but as a foreigner with no communication skills, I would never understand. Even though I didn't know these people, I felt their sorrow, so I moved on quickly.

However, the attempt to escape sadness resulted in the opposite, as I passed a man lying on the ground with no legs. As I came closer, I saw that he had lost an arm as well. He was begging for money with an empty tin can placed in front of him. His eyes followed me close, touching my heart like a dog begging for food. Was it right of me to feel so sad for myself when people were suffering like that? Nothing could bring his limbs back - nothing could give him a normal life - nothing could prevent him from being a cripple until his death. The money I picked from my pocket and placed in the tin can wouldn't do much other than feed him for a couple of weeks, but he thanked me with a genuine grin. This time my own smile was wide as the man sent me a flying kiss and a wink. Amazed by the positivity of this man, I laughed, caught his kiss in the air and placed it in my pocket. The man laughed with me. His laughter was loud as I told him goodbye and continued my search for coffee.

Minutes later, I still couldn't stop wondering how this man stayed so positive. Maybe he had just gotten a bit insane. But even so, wasn't his happiness not true? At the end of the day, everything we experience is nothing but our own perception of the world around us, right? What is our existence really? Does life actually have a meaning? Is there an afterlife? Maybe Violet was watching me from some divine place? Was she sitting with some god?

I stopped myself from developing more silly questions. I must have been tired, and even moved my hand up to check on the two missing fingers, but they were still on my hand. Well, why would my missing fingers hunt me in my dreams? As I bend the fingers, I felt them crack like they used to. Why did this dream feel more like reality? I turned my head and glanced at the disabled man in the distance. He was still watching me, still laughing happily. At that moment, I became unsure of what was real and what was not. Was Violet even dead? Of course she was. I would never see her again. Never hug her. Never listen to her sweet voice. I would never have more time with her. What good is time when there's nothing to enjoy anymore? Wha…

"Coffee?" a woman asked from her little yellow stall, pulling me out of my depressing thoughts.

"Yes, please," I exhaled. "I need coffee."

Chapter 18

My heart raced as our sprinting increased to unbelievable speed. The shadow was in front of us, trying to slow us down by releasing rocks from the ceiling. To some degree, it was working, but Lumit was swift in removing the hundreds of rocks and stones, continually raining down in front of us. Running ahead of me, she threw handful after handful of metallic powder up the air, moving her arms, resulting in the rocks being pushed to the side. The glittering effect was mesmerizing, making me doubt if I was dreaming or if this was actually real. Inhaling the powder might have played a role in this.

Lumit slowed down just enough for me to reach her, before she handed me an empty glass orb. I almost dropped it, as it was burning hot, but managed to grab Pete's brown pouch from my pocket and hold the orb with the fabric.

"When I order, throw it at the evil!" Lumit commanded.

My body filled with anxiety. I didn't feel confident enough to pull this off. I would fail again. Everything was happening too fast. I didn't understand what was happening. Lumit started mumbling a mantra while speeding up. She threw a bunch of golden sticks out the air, which kept hovering in front of her, glowing bright by the reflection of my torch. The sticks formed a hexagon and initiated a rotating movement, only increasing in speed. I heard the shadow screech, creating trembling vibrations, making the hairs in my neck rise. A thin trail of blackness formed between the shadow and the hexagon. I realized that a familiar bright light revealed itself in the distance; Sunlight! The exit was close. This was it; We had *one* chance of capturing the orb and sealing the exit. We had to succeed!

"A little closer!" Lumit shouted.

It shouldn't be possible, but we managed to speed up, getting closer to the shadow - but the exit was closing in just as fast, and our time was running out. I felt the orb getting colder the nearer we came to the sunlight, and the fresh air was cooling my sweating skin down.

The next moment, I was freezing on the outside, but burning up inside, like a killing fever. My lungs were burning, but my breaths were ice. The sunlight was blinding, as we almost reached the exit. We were nearly out of time. We had to act now - and Lumit knew that. She lifted her hand, pushing the rotating hexagon fast forward. The shadow screeched.

"Now, Christian! Throw the orb!"

dream

A ray of sunshine forced my eyes open. I was sitting on a two-step stairway a bit outside the vault. How long had I been sitting there? I rubbed my tired eyes and checked my phone; No news from the others. They were still planning in the hotel room.

I observed the vault entrance. It was hard to grasp that we were *this* close to unimaginable wealth. The key to eliminating The Power was right behind those doors - but behind those guards as well. I still couldn't believe that the vault was *that* protected; I counted eight guards, half of them loaded with firearms, half of them being monks with eyes like hawks. There was no way to get past so many. It was a tough idea to give up now without battle, but I was out of energy.

One of the monks appeared alerted and examined the vault door. It attracted the attention of two other guards, who also moved their eyes to the door. It gave me hope of distracting the guards, but realizing that the five other guards were purposely watching the surroundings killed the hope just as fast. The monk found a stick and slammed it down the ground a couple of times. It turned out to be nothing but a rat stealing their attention for a moment, and then all eight were back on duty. Impossible. What was I thinking? Did I seriously believe that the four of us could defeat such tremendous power? Did I really assume that we could convince people that their beloved heroes were, in fact, the enemy? I had been so naive. What did it all matter anyway?

Violet would never come back. I would never feel true happiness again. I was a complete failure.

The little pouch from Pete fell out of my pocket. Checking its content, I found that it was filled with pills; The medicine that our children needed. Pete said it was to remind me that what we were doing was good, but now that our plans were impossible, being reminded only hurt. I just sat there staring at the pills. I was dreaming, right? What would happen if I swallowed these pills? Would dying in a dream result in awakening? So I would wake up, escape the vault and see my daughter again. Wasn't she alive in reality? *Wasn't she?* My head was spinning.

I stared at the pills for a while, reflecting, with the necklace in my hand… Violet's necklace…

Chapter 19

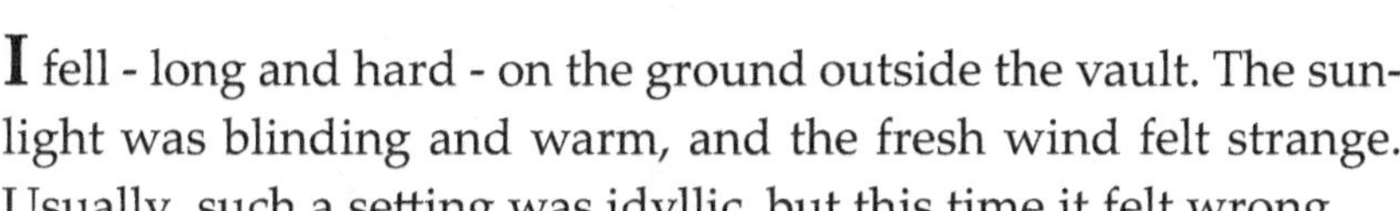

I fell - long and hard - on the ground outside the vault. The sunlight was blinding and warm, and the fresh wind felt strange. Usually, such a setting was idyllic, but this time it felt wrong.

Lumit was nowhere to be seen as I got up from the ground. Neither did I see the shadow. Only a few strange guards were idling in the distance. They didn't see me. I wanted to call out for them but noticed the orb in my hand. I realized that it was cold as ice, opened my hand and dropped it. But as it hit the ground, it became an empty, brown pouch. It seemed surreal. The whole world seemed surreal. I tried pinching my arm, just like whenever I wanted to dream inside the vault, but this time the dream wouldn't come. For a split second, I saw myself standing in the vault entrance, from behind the guards. But the dream wouldn't let me keep dreaming. I was stuck in this unreal reality.

I looked out the horizon. The sky was turning dark. Not only dark - but black. Deep black. I didn't make it in time. It won. *It fucking won again!* I couldn't believe it. This was the end. This time there was no one to save me; No one to save children like Violet; No one to save the world.

The blackening sky was coming close, absorbing all light on the ground, creating nothing but shadow. The guards disappeared, dissolving into grains of black. I felt my heart beating slower. My feet became numb. The ground in front disappeared, my heart beating slower. The darkness devoured me, swallowing me whole, starting from my feet and up - heart beating slower. Everything turned black. The whole world stopped spinning. Nothing existed anymore. My heart stopped.

Time was never a problem, after all.

Epilogue

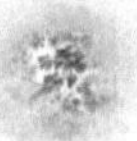

Mona ended the call, grabbed her pen and wrote some notes on a piece of paper. She shook her head in denial, letting the frustration rush through her body. Then she put the pen down, turned in her chair and looked out the window. The sun was shining bright on the blue sky. The birds were twittering through the open window, which also allowed the refreshing breeze to cool her down. "How did the world become so horrible?" she thought. "Why did we allow that to happen?"

She turned to her laptop, continuing the visual research she was doing for the new line of posters. The images were horrible, but she had to go through it. Watching pictures was not as hard as being out there in person. A tear escaped her eye. She just couldn't hold it back. But she had to continue - this was bigger than her.

When she heard footsteps walking down the stairs, she paused and waited for them to move to her side. Christian kissed her on the chin and smiled, but Mona didn't settle with that and took him in for a genuine love kiss, blushing like never before. She informed him that Pete, Mia and Max just called; They had gathered the new evidence, but needed a day off, as the conditions out there were too horrible. Christian nodded;

"They are doing well, of course they should have a day off," he said. "Let them have a week if they need it."

Mona stood up and went in for a hug. Both of them enjoyed every single one of the twenty seconds of embracement.

"Oh, and the press called," Mona informed after ending the hug. "They want another interview."

"Very well. I'll call them later."

One month earlier, the world received news of a Canadian man swallowing a handful of pills in the middle of an Indian street. The man died but was revived in the hospital, even though the doctors predicted it impossible. First, the story went viral, as many people suggested it was the curse of the Vault causing the man to commit suicide. Christian later told his story, along with the nerds' information, and another round of news spread - faster than the medical industry could control with its wealth. In the end, the community of the little town formed a resistance and fought the industry. The truth was revealed while it turned out that the facility already had a cure, only to be used by the important employees. The facility was shut down, eliminating the release of hazardous smog, and the children of the town all received the cure. Everyone involved in The Power was convicted of murder to children, receiving the worst penalty the town had ever seen. The little society was changed. Christian, Mona and the three geeks formed an organization whose purpose was to reveal and bust large industries, and to help the world see the truth. Thanks to Violet's interest in sea animals, a particular food industry was now the target, and Christian was determined to enlighten the world of their ignorance. It was only a matter of time before the world would be taken back by the population.

Christian had stopped taking antidepressants, or "vitamins" as his doctor described them, which became a part of his life a month before Violet's death, and now he felt energized like never before. The antidepressants were prescribed for him during an annual cholesterol check; Not because Christian needed it, but because the doctor was paid to prescribe certain drugs, he found. Now Christian knew what was real and what wasn't. He wasn't confused anymore.

Picking up his brown coffee mug, he went outside in the sun. In the front yard, he heard a familiar voice greet him behind the newly planted, short hedge. The neighbor stood with a bunch of colorful balloons, hovering from strings in his hand.

"Oh, hello there, Bob," Christian greeted. "Why the balloons?"

"It's today, Christian," the neighbor, Bob, giggled. "The wife and I have been off the cigarettes for a month. We're celebrating."

Christian smiled, happy to hear about the achievement.

"You deserve that, my friend. By the way, I found the chainsaw you requested. Just come by when you need it."

"I will, my man."

When Christian was transported from India to Canada, the neighbor had just returned home from another trip to Dubai; A journey that would help both him and the wife to quit smoking. The neighbors came by the caravan in which Christian and Mona had moved since selling the house. They brought coffee and homemade, healthy, vegan cakes. Bob and the wife turned out to be surprisingly friendly. The annoying smirk was nothing but a timid smile, and when Christian thought about it, Bob had only been talking about his first Dubai trip twice. The wife was still a bit too talkative for his taste, but nothing he couldn't tolerate. Mona liked the talking better.

As the evening progressed, and the four befriended, a pact was formed; Bob and the wife were to help Christian and Mona get their house back. Christian urged to return to the house, as he missed the memories of Violet it contained. After The Power was busted, the wealth was shared between affected people, including the medicine-customers who had their money back. It meant that Christian and Mona had money to rebuy their house. But there was a problem; The new owners wouldn't move. Well, only until Bob made his *evil master plan*, as he called it. The plan worked, and the new owners fled the area and put the house on sale. "*Who knew that this friendly guy could be that much a pain in the ass,*" Christian giggled to himself. He still felt that he was in huge debt to Bob, but Bob denied and laughed: "Who wouldn't want a famous neighbor?" What a guy.

"Okay, Bob, I have to get back inside," Christian said. "See you at our Wednesday-morning run tomorrow - seven-thirty, right?

"Bet ya!"

He returned inside and sat down next to Mona. They kissed and shared a smile. A picture of Violet stood on the desk, next to the calendar. She shared her beautiful smile with her parents.

"See you tonight, Violet," Christian whispered. "We'll continue our song in my dream."

Acknowledgement

We all live in a world full of information. Nevertheless, there are still unanswered questions, and facts which people disagree upon; What are dreams? What is the meaning of life? What happens when we die?

Most of us believe in the facts we hear, even though we never saw any evidence ourselves. We trust in the words of "experts" - who might or might not be telling the truth, since many factors can influence the results - like money, for example.

This book was written to remind myself how important it is to think for yourself, use your eyes and not trust in everything. It has been an exciting journey, and I hope that you enjoyed reading the outcome.

I want to thank every single one who read this book. Publishing books isn't the same without you. A huge acknowledgment to my family for being the best people in the world, and to my partner who took the time to help me out refining this book.

I love to get feedback, whether it's positive or negative. Please feel free to mail me at mill@millwoods.eu. As a return, you are welcome to request a free copy of my next ebook.

Best Regards
Mill Woods

More by Mill Woods

If you liked reading this book, here is something for you.

Two Lives, One Adventure
is a romantic adventure story
about love, freedom and plausible
mysterious magic.

*A joyful novel that will stay
with you forever.*

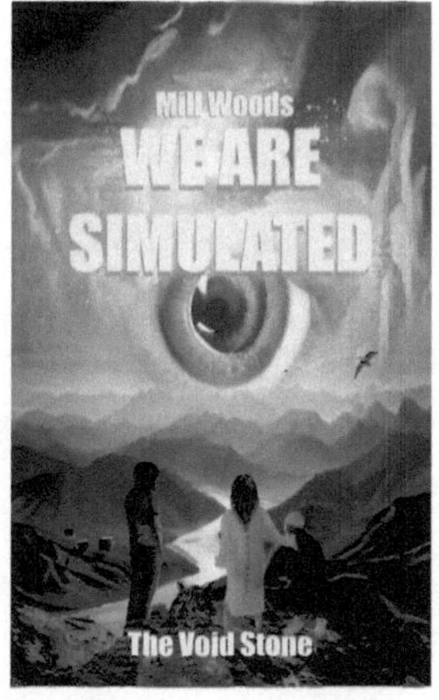

We are Simulated (series)
is a heart-pounding tale of fri-
endship, resilience, and the
quest for truth in a simulated
reality on the verge of collapse.

*Will Koa and his friends unravel
the mysteries of the simulation
and emerge victorious, or will
their world forever be altered by
the unseen forces?*

* 9 7 8 8 7 9 7 1 8 1 9 4 2 *